For the "Hesitating Purchaser
or
the "Curious Browser"

"Written in sincerity,
With clarity and brevity,
Using integrity,
To safeguard the identity,
Of each and every entity,
While creating some hilarity,
And causing lots of levity,
It centres on the destiny,
We reach before posterity."

Mr and Mrs Pensioner a Lancashire couple who after many years of marriage, have recently retired and are looking forward to "spending time and doing things – together".

However the destiny which everyone hopes to obtain is beset with difficulties and marred by misfortune — or is it?

Acknowledgements

I am indebted to the following for all of their help, advice and support.

To the various relatives, friends, acquaintances and adversaries who in their own way have all made vital contributions to this book – A huge "Thank You" because your actions and words made it possible.

To the Welsh Books Council for the support - I am truly grateful.

To Mark Knopfler for the inspiration – my sincere appreciation.

To the entire team at JimEriddles for the superb advice and guidance – Please accept my heartfelt gratitude.

To Annie – the biggest "Thank You" possible for everything over the last 45 years but especially for Laura and Chris.

For Harry Jack,

"You can track,
Young Harry Jack,
As he explores,
The great outdoors."

Prologue.

"What's written here, is almost true,

With names changed so they cannot sue,

But if some say, "I think it's you",

Who's depicted from page two,

I'll reply, "I thought you knew",

Then list- just who - it could be too,

And for those who haven't a clue,

What I'm saying or trying to do,

Please don't start feeling blue,

Or get yourself in a stew,

Cos really you have nought to rue,

You don't even have to queue,

For the knowledge you'll accrue,

When I explain - just who's - who."

Our First Year in Pensionland

by

Mr Pensioner

Chapter One

"The Goal"

"Both being born in Lancashire,
Is not the only thing we share,
It was the first step on our way,
That led us to this crucial day,
Ladders crossed, in our teens,
Going steady and all that means,
To be engaged was our next rung,
Soon church bells were being rung,
Kids were on the upper tread,
We soon had two - being fed,
Then the years went flying by,
Where did they go? We'd often sigh,
Now and then we may have faltered,
But our stairway never altered,
While all the time collecting cares,
We'd carry on - climbing stairs,
Then the kids flew our nest,
Still no time to stop or rest,
But now our work is at an end,
And only "our" needs to attend,
Cos they say we've reached old age,
Ascended to the final stage,
Even though we are much wiser,
Retirement's top of our next riser,
But as we mount the higher flight,
We hatch a plan to make it right,
An' all we need to finish our climb,
Is lots of one another's time."

Mrs Pensioner looked at me and I looked at Mrs Pensioner, "Well, what now?" she asked.

We had woken at the usual time, washed, dressed, had breakfast and watched the early morning news on TV – all as normal. Everything was the same; exactly the same, this was the identical routine that we had gone through every working day since the kids left home. Next, we would go to work - me to the engineering factory and Mrs Pensioner to her nursing duties - jobs we had both been doing since leaving school all those years ago.

Except today was different - so very different, there was no work, we had retired - and this was the first day of the rest of our lives.

"What now," she repeated, obviously thinking that I had gone deaf overnight – just because I was now officially, a pensioner.

"Well it's not raining," I observed, "so what about a walk?"

That's how our lives in Pensionland began, both of us going through a ritual we had performed thousands of times before. At the time I thought it a little strange, particularly as we had discussed on many occasions our hopes and aspirations for that momentous day and of course all of the other days which we hoped still lay ahead of us.

"Take up golf, go fishing, fly to Australia, get fit, travel round Britain, lose weight, use our bus passes, visit museums" all had been listed, considered and quantified. Then we realised that none of our ambitions could provide the feelings of excitement or elation we anticipated unless they were accomplished by both of us – doing them together.

So what could prevent us from achieving this very simple objective of being together?

Well like everyone else, we had little control over our health and even less influence regarding our lifespan, two factors which could destroy our plans at any time.

No further thought was needed, "spending time and doing things – together" became our goal and whether we were replacing floor beams, digging out trees, relaying cobble stones, knocking down walls or simply walking, we would always try to do it - **together**.

Now, over twelve months later, has our objective changed?
No, definitely not, we still do things together but nowadays in a very controlled and careful manner.

So why the change to a more cautious approach?

Well for the answer, you will have to read my story but it is sufficient to say I have only chosen to disclose the facts concerning one incident, from each month of Our First Year in Pensionland.

So please read on......

Retirement

Lancashire

Mr Pensioner

Chapter Two

January

"A Day in Therapy"

"Powder by the sprinkle,
Mix it with war paint,
Makes the little wrinkle,
Appear as if it ain't,

Cleansing with a lotion,
Rubbing with a cream,
Stirring any potion,
To recreate the dream,

Now she's using fish,
And they're not from any tin,
Hope she's got her wish,
Cos they're eating all her skin."

For the last 40 years Mrs Pensioner has tried to stop time or more accurately, halt the ravages of time.

In her quest for eternal youth she has tried countless potions and creams. At one point, I thought our home had become a warehouse for Oil of Ulay because we possessed so much of the stuff. We had night cream, day cream, anti-ageing, anti-wrinkle, re-energising, as well as the full range of moisturisers and cleansers to produce the "total effect".

I remember very well that momentous day when Ulay became Olay; for weeks it was thought because the "U" in Ulay had been transformed into an "O" for Olay a significant break-through in the search for everlasting beauty had been achieved. Putting two and two together, Mrs Pensioner thought that Olay was the English spelling of the Spanish word "Olé", which after consulting a Spanish dictionary she learned was a, "cry of triumph or achievement".

I suppose it is quite easy to see how her misinterpretation occurred but she believed the manufacturers of Olay had discovered the magic elixir and were secretly telling everyone of their triumph. Everyone that is, who bothered to consult an English/Spanish dictionary!

I really hadn't got the heart to tell her that the name change was made purely for copyright reasons and that the stuff in the jars was exactly the same whether it was spelt with a "U" or an "O". Nevertheless, ever since "transformation" day or "O" day as it became known in our house, the kids were ordered to buy Olay for her Birthday, Christmas, or Mother's Day presents and slowly our large stock of Ulay was replaced.

I suppose it was a bit like when a Marathon bar became a Snickers bar they were exactly the same under the wrapper but Mrs P always said I preferred a marathon.

I digress however, so returning to my tale, hard skin has always been Mrs P's nemesis and to be more precise, hard skin on her feet. Over the years she has tried foot spas, pedeggs, pedicures, pumice stones and every other treatment imaginable, as well as applying an abundance of the aforesaid creams, potions, lotions, oils and powders.

Yet nothing worked!

Well that is to say nothing worked to her satisfaction.

Take the foot spa; a Christmas present from the kids, it was used twice and on both occasions water bubbled all over the bedroom carpet. Now it is back in its box at the bottom of our wardrobe and presumably waiting for the Antiques Roadshow to come around.

I can see it now; it will be just like when the expert takes one of those old tinplate toys out of its box. All of the oohs, aahs and cries of astonishment with the connoisseur saying, "What wonderful condition, you must have really looked after it, and still in its original box". "No scratches or marks, the collectors will pay a lot for one as perfect as this and with the authentic packaging – well, the sky is the limit – you can name your own price."

The only problem I can see for my get rich scheme is that thousands and thousands must have been sold and more than likely they are all back in the box at the bottom of the owner's wardrobe.

Dr Scholl, now that was another favourite manufacturer of Mrs P.

Over the years, she must have tested all of their products and I still recall those happy times spent with Dr Scholl's "Smooth My Sole" micro file. It had a stainless steel blade which the good doctor promised wouldn't burst a balloon. Do you remember in the advertisement they had a woman using the file on a big red balloon and miraculously it didn't burst – the balloon that is.

What was the point of a stainless steel blade incapable of busting a balloon yet fitted to a file?

I still can't quite understand the logic; I would have thought that if it can't burst a balloon then it won't be capable of filing hard skin because the skin on Mrs P's feet is a lot harder than any balloon.

I would have advertised the blade as, "being made of the hardest metal known to man – guaranteed to cut anything." Then show the file cutting through a huge steel hawser that fastened the QE 2 to the dockside.

Now that would have convinced a few women suffering from hard skin to buy it.

The file also claimed to be "ergonomically designed to fit in a woman's hand".

It always struck me, how do they know a woman is going to use it and which woman's hand was it designed for? Even I know that all women's hands are not the same. Take Mrs Bridge from number 62, she is over eighteen stone with hands the size of coal shovels, yet young, newlywed Mrs Dawson from across the road is tiny and needs both hands to hold a wine glass.

So what size of woman's hand was the "Smooth My Sole" file ergonomically designed for?

Not that it matters anymore because the "file" is now filed away alongside the foot spa, where I am hoping they will stay, happy together, forever and ever.

With all the grief and aggravation received from Mrs P, I always claimed that she should concentrate on "soothing her soul" rather than "smoothing her sole" anyway.

Today however was the day for her latest experiment and to make matters worse because of our objective of "doing things together" I was now included in her plans and to be honest, I wasn't looking forward to it!

My services had been "booked" 3 weeks previously and the date was carved on my brain - Friday the 28th.

Even if World War Three was to break out, I wouldn't be able to attend because today I had a prior engagement - an appointment, which couldn't possibly be broken.

Golf, walking, fishing, drinking all had been banned because today I was reserved exclusively for the whim of Mrs P.

During the previous few weeks I had tried everything to be released from my obligation but nothing it seemed could change her plans. I had even offered to "bring the garden up to scratch" by spending the whole day, mowing, cutting, digging and hoeing, only to be told that it was the wrong time of the year for that type of gardening.

Undeterred, I had suggested treating our garden fences with 2 coats of creosote only to be informed that the preservative had been banned since 2003 on Health and Safety grounds

"How the hell can we stop our fence from rotting if we can't use creosote?" I had asked, secretly hoping that I could paint the fence with whatever answer she came up with.

"WE use Fence Preserve" she replied indignantly, before adding, "It is environmentally friendly and doesn't harm plants or animals".

"That sounds good stuff", I responded optimistically, "I'll paint the fence with that."

"It was done 2 weeks ago and I DID IT as usual, while you were out playing golf in the Men's Competition," Mrs P had replied somewhat curtly.

Changing tact, I moved my attentions indoors, "the hall and stairs could do with a lick of paint", I observed.

"Yes I know and I have arranged for Peter the Painter to do it next month," came the terse reply.

It was no use, there was no way out, I had to do what a man has been told to do.

I had to drive Mrs P to her fish treatment appointment.

This therapy had been recommended to her a couple of months previously by her friend Freda or "Big F," as I call her (but only when I am out of earshot).

According to Big F, not only did the treatment remove all of her unwanted skin, it also reduced her stress levels, giving her a "peaceful feeling of serene tranquillity".

Now as you have probably guessed, I am totally in favour of a stress free Mrs P and one with skin as smooth as a baby's bottom is definitely a bonus but the £45 charge for the 45 minute treatment was something I was completely against.

£1 a minute!!

Now that's what I call expensive and what's more, the therapy doesn't claim to cure a patient forever and ever, which means you are expected to return again for another dose!

So having the previous experience of all of the other treatments that had never worked and me constantly reminding her of all of the failed gadgets stored in our wardrobe, I had managed to persuade Mrs P to stay away.

That is until the dreaded 30% off leaflet dropped through our letter box.

Much to my disappointment I was out golfing (in another men only competition) that fateful day, so when I arrived home (already in a bad mood because of a poor round) the deed was done an appointment had been made and I was the designated driver.

When "take off" time finally arrived I drove her as slowly as possible and with the utmost care to her fishy rendezvous. I must have driven exceptionally well because I can only remember receiving three mild rebukes and one serious reprimand during the whole journey.

In retrospect, there was a second reprimand but I don't think it really counts because I collected it whilst stopped and after parking.

So having delivered Mrs P safely to the city centre, I accompanied her to the therapy centre to satisfy our aspiration of "doing things together." I hope it goes without saying that I wasn't expected to undergo the treatment because going with her was punishment enough and completely fulfilled the criterion of our objective.

Once inside the beautifully decorated "Therapy Centre" (I reflected that at £1 a minute they could afford to have the place looking plush) Mrs P was led away to have her feet washed while I was made comfortable in the reception area.

While waiting, I took the opportunity of doing some research by speaking to the very attractive receptionist who "helpfully" gave me some pamphlets to read.

Apparently the fish treatment consists of fish actually eating human skin! The patients sit on glorified benches dangling their feet into a tank of warm water, then the fish attack and eat all of the hard skin!

"This I must see" I thought, mentally visualising small sharks gnawing away at Mrs P's feet.

You can imagine my disappointment when I actually saw the fish and they were only about an inch long!

"They are totally useless," I muttered under my breath.

Then turning to the therapist, I informed her that she had completely underestimated the size of the task. It required at least two dozen Piranhas, which should have completed an intensive training course with the SAS before being allowed to tackle Mrs P's feet!

I had the feeling that she had heard similar comments before because she just smiled at me ever so serenely before handing me more information leaflets. She obviously thought I could be fully occupied by reading and therefore unable to pester her anymore.

So I took the hint and read.

It seems the fish are called Doctor Fish but their scientific name is Gara Rufa Fish and they are from the warm waters of Turkey. Normally there are about 200 in a tank and they don't have teeth but use their gums to nibble and suck away the hard skin. It is the combination of warm water and the tingling effect produced by the fish that reduces patient's stress levels.

I thought that it sounded a bit like underwater acupuncture. Then I read, "The water is constantly filtered to prevent con-tamination". I wasn't sure if the filters were to prevent the fish from being contaminated or the patients but I wouldn't risk asking.

The expensive 45 minutes ticked away and by the look on Mrs P face she seemed to be enjoying the whole experience.

Meanwhile having read every available pamphlet and brochure, I was fast becoming a leading authority on Doctor Fish and my mind was beginning to wander –

"Who the hell found out in the first place that Gara Rufa fish eat dry, hard, human skin?"

"Who discovered that they reduced stress levels?"

"How do these people learn these things?"

"Have they dipped their toes into tanks full of every type of fish in the world?"

"Having found a capable fish, how did they know the treatment could be sold as a remedy?"

While I was still ruminating on these and many other questions, my brain drifted even further -

"If I had been told 30 years ago that one day, I would be sat in the City Centre watching my wife being eaten alive by fish with no teeth and she was not only staying very calm about it but also paying an exorbitant fee for the privilege."

Well, would you have believed it!!

There was only about five minutes left of Mrs P's session when she was joined on the bench by a rather large, stout lady.

The two exchanged pleasantries before the newcomer very warily and extremely hesitantly lowered her legs into the "soothing" water. Her feet could only have been in the tank for a few seconds when emitting a low gurgling sound, she passed out, keeled over and fell forwards towards her tank.

Realising the gravity of the situation, Mrs P made a valiant attempt to stop her but a combination of the woman's weight and Mrs P being restrained by her own tank made any rescue impossible. Plunging headlong from the bench the woman's knees caught the top of her tank, tipping it over and spilling water and fish everywhere.

She lay motionless for a few seconds, her head on the floor and her legs on top of the upturned tank with water soaking into her clothes and fish wriggling all around her.

Mrs P reached her first, followed closely by the therapist and myself. I wanted to pull the woman to her feet but Mrs P with her nurse's instinct kicking in, managed to stop me. She turned the woman onto her side, checked that her airway was clear and began taking her pulse.

The therapist meanwhile had run off leaving me to salvage the fish, which when captured, I placed carefully into the tank recently vacated by Mrs P.

After about a minute or so the woman began to recover and as I continued to rescue the fish, she told Mrs P her story.

Apparently she never wanted the treatment because she had a phobia about fish, not the type with batter on obviously, just the wriggling sort. As a child she had been holidaying in Morecambe Bay and while paddling in the shallows, she inadvertently stood on a flat fish that was resting in the mud. The sensation of it squirming to escape from the trap that was the underside of her foot was something she could never forget and even now the sight of a wriggling fish had a detrimental effect on her.

In normal circumstances she would never have agreed to the treatment but at Christmas she had been given a voucher as a present. Consequently, under a lot of pressure she had reluctantly consented to use the voucher but to make matters worse because of her nervousness she had not eaten anything that day.

Mrs P had just finished telling her that she must eat something as soon as possible and I had retrieved all of the fish I could find, apart from the one I believe the therapist stood on, when the receptionist told us that an ambulance had been summoned.

So with the situation improving and help on the way, I suggested to Mrs P that it was time for us to leave but just then the woman let out an ear-splitting scream and began tearing at her sodden skirt.

From deep within its folds dropped a wriggling fish, closely followed by another. With the skirt off and on the floor, the woman now crying began to remove her top.

Thinking that this Big City behaviour was a bit too much for a village bloke from Lancashire, I beat a hasty retreat to the reception area, leaving Mrs P to deal with the now semi-nude, hysterical woman.

Ten minutes later with the woman now much calmer and sipping very sweet tea, I again recommended to Mrs P that we should leave.

Desperately trying to recover the situation, the receptionist attempted to persuade Mrs P to finish the treatment but in the end settled for giving us both Free Treatment Vouchers as a gesture of "thanks" for our help.

As we were going through the door to leave, I suggested - much too loudly - that they should consider fitting seat belts to the benches to prevent any recurrence of the incident.

During our journey home my mind began to wander again;- "If I had been told 30 years ago that one day, I would be sat in the City Centre, watching my wife being eaten alive by fish with no teeth and she was not only staying very calm about it but also paying an exorbitant fee for the privilege, then I would be saving those same fish by scraping them off the floor while my wife attended to an almost nude, panic-stricken woman."

Well, would you have believed it!!

When we finally arrived home, the vouchers were placed on the hall table and that's where they remain, untouched to this day!

Mrs P still continues with her quest for the magic elixir of youth but her enthusiasm for fish therapy has completely disappeared and to my utter amazement, I now take a very keen interest.

For whenever I pass one of the fish treatment centres (and they are becoming very popular nowadays) I always look to see if my Health and Safety advice has been heeded by checking for those essential seat belts.

As I said to Mrs P, I don't believe that particular type of pedicure will be "toe-tally" safe until they are installed in every therapy centre throughout the world.

Chapter Three

February

"Romantic Semantics"

"Often described as pedantic,
And never considered romantic,
Could I alter perception?
Without causing deception,
And if so, what could I buy?
For a little romance to imply,

In the past a bottle of Olay,
Had always been thought of as OK,
But today, I thought - "No!"
She needs something more,
So I continued to think,
Of coats made from mink,
And flowers that were subtly pink,
I even threw in a new sink,
But would she possibly settle,
For a gift made from sheet metal,
And if so, we need a new **kettle!**

So that's how I got the idea,
Don't know what made it appear,
But now, it's clear as a bell,
There's nothing more to tell,
So never get anxious or frantic,
Even if you're slightly pedantic,
Cos' a kettle is always romantic."

Valentine's Day was fast approaching and in years gone by I had always been heavily criticised for not buying that special Valentine gift.

Well to be perfectly honest, I was usually condemned as "not having one romantic bone in my body".

Previously I had always made the excuse that I did not have enough time to go to the shops because of work.

This year however, I thought I couldn't possibly get away with that explanation and as I couldn't think of any plausible justification on which to base my defence, I had with great reluctance, started to consider suitable presents.

Flowers came easily to mind but what was the point, they would be dead within a week and then binned. Did this mean my romantic gesture would also suffer the same fate and be dead, disposed of and forgotten within the week?

No, if I was going to break the habit of a lifetime then my passionate action had to be something unforgettable, something so amazing that it would save me from ever having to provide anything even vaguely romantic ever again. It had to be so incredible that it would make me immune from any disapproval whatsoever – well as far as romance was concerned that is. It must be so good that it would only need the merest mention to put me on a pedestal alongside Romeo, Mr Darcy or even Saint Valentine himself.

I decided to go to the local library to do some research and I learned that the Taj Mahal is considered to be the most romantic gift ever.

Apparently it was built by some Shah, as a monument to his wife who had just died giving birth to their fourteenth child. I soon abandoned any such notions, thinking Mrs P was bit past giving birth to another twelve children, plus my brick laying skills weren't that good and where in Lancashire would I find that amount of white marble?

So deciding to go back to basics, I searched for the correct definition of "Romantic" but that was when my troubles really began because there is no agreement on what it actually means.

It was variously defined as; - an event, an atmosphere, a heroic quality, an imaginative quality, mysterious, idealised, quixotic, a love affair and one even described it as **"conducive to, or suitable for lovemaking"**.

If the books couldn't decide on a meaning, what chance had I got of buying a romantic present when nobody could tell me what the word really meant?

With my head spinning I was about to give up, when by sheer good luck, I found the following statement: - "romantic is a very vague and imprecise mood or feeling with the curious property of being describable but not definable."

I began to feel a little better, reasoning that if no one could define "Romantic" then how would anybody know if my gift was romantic or not? All I had to do was describe it as my "romantic present" and nobody could possibly argue otherwise - could they?

Not wishing to take any risks I decided to investigate further, after all this was my big chance; I could score full marks on the romance front and even pick up some extra bonus points, provided I donated a suitable offering. So, believing my time would be well invested, I explored the mysteries of romance even further and I soon discovered that certain things could be considered romantic. Very low lighting is high on the list, with candles even higher, so taking Mrs P for a late night meal, then removing all of the restaurant's bulbs and replacing with one single candle could be an answer.

Except my hypothesis regarding the flowers being dead within a week could be applied here because once the meal was eaten that was the end of it and what's more, I hate it when I can't see what I am eating.

I also learned that the colour red is romantic, as are certain "cute" items, such as teddy bears or puppies.

What Mrs P would have done with a bright red, stuffed, teddy bear? God only knows, probably have stuffed it up my *******. As for puppies, well I have never seen a red one but I didn't think it appropriate, not with all the possible mess on the carpet, she would have to be cleaning constantly.

Absorbed in my research I discovered that centuries ago, the word "romantic" probably meant "to make love like the Romans". Having watched Up Pompeii and the more recent adventures of Spartacus, I thought Mrs P wouldn't totally appreciate an orgy, not at her age. So somewhat reluctantly, I removed it from my list of possibilities. Then I read that "Romantic" could also be classified according to two categories, "popular romance" and "divine or spiritual romance".

I wasn't sure what was meant exactly by "divine or spiritual" but I certainly wasn't going to get involved with ghosts or anything religious because I have enough trouble with the Jehovah's Witnesses when they come knocking on our door.

"Popular romance," now I thought I knew what they meant by that. Could it be all of those Mills and Boon books? Should I have been reading those all along, instead of wasting my time with all of the intellectual stuff?

As a result I spent most of the following week trawling my way through two of their great works but the only helpful suggestion I found worth contemplating was my possible suicide. So giving up, (on Mills and Boon that is) I continued to rack my brain for inspiration.

I remembered a work colleague many years ago telling me that he had bought his wife a car for Valentine's Day. He had paid extra for it to be delivered in the dead of night and left on their driveway complete with a pink ribbon fastened around it.

Evidently when his wife opened the curtains next morning all was pure joy and ecstasy.

What a pity I thought, when I learned of their divorce only six months later.

Joe down at the club told me that through his computer, he had booked a weekend in Paris for him and his wife. She had no idea where she was going until they arrived at Manchester Airport. Surprisingly, she was furious when she learned of their destination because, "she had not brought any suitable clothes".

Women, who can understand them?

However, neither of those proposals could be solutions to my problem because:-

A) With my luck, we would be stuck at Manchester Airport due to fog or some strike or other and

B) I did not have the authority to spend the amount of money needed for flights or cars without Mrs P's prior knowledge or permission.

As a consequence I had to continue with my quest but at least I was now armed with the knowledge that my gift had to be small and relatively inexpensive. That's when I turned my attention to the kitchen.

The food mixer, microwave, pans, scales, even the kitchen sink, were all fairly new and in perfect working order. Then it hit me – the kettle – Mrs P had pointed out only a few weeks previously that it had sprung the tiniest of leaks.

Was this condemnation of our kettle, Woman's Code for, "buy me a new kettle for Valentine's Day?

It had to be, why tell **me** about a faulty kettle, if it wasn't?

A huge sense of relief came flooding over me and I slept better that night than I had done in weeks.

The next day was the fourteenth and after a quick trip to our local appliance shop, I had the kettle. There wasn't that many to choose from – not in my price range and they all do the same job don't they?

So what was the point of paying sixty quid for one, when the one I bought cost less than twenty?

I found some almost new, brown paper to wrap it in and on that I wrote, "Happy Valentine's Day" with a big, black, felt tip pen.

Feeling pretty pleased with myself, I awaited the return of Mrs P who having gone to meet an old friend was due back around teatime. "It would be perfect timing", I thought, "As she is making our meal, I can give her my present".

That is exactly what happened, the meal was almost cooked and as she took hold of our old kettle to fill and plug it in, I gave her the brown paper wrapped box saying, "Happy Valentine's Day".

I still don't know what I did wrong but it was obvious that she was quite upset about something.

At first I thought she must have heard some bad news from her friend earlier in the day but no, it was definitely something about the kettle that was troubling her.

I offered to change it for another model, adding that I still had the receipt. My suggestion only seemed to make matters worse because she stormed from the kitchen with tears trickling down her face, leaving our food to go cold on the worktop.

For the next hour or so the atmosphere was definitely cold, frosty even, as I tried desperately to discover the problem. Unfortunately everything I said appeared to aggravate the situation, so with relationships deteriorating rapidly, I decided not to say anything else.

We sat in complete silence for the next half hour and then she muttered something, which I couldn't quite hear but sounded like, "shouldn't have expected anything else after forty years."

Then still sniffling, she returned to the kitchen and began re-heating our food. I foolhardily proposed using our new kettle for the drinks and after giving me one of her most withering glares, she took the stainless steel vessel from its box for the first time.

Very carefully it was filled and plugged in but when she flicked the switch to turn it on, our kitchen light went out. Not only that but all of our lights went out, the cooker went off, in fact everything electrical went off.

I couldn't see Mrs P but I knew instantly she wasn't pleased and all I heard was, "Bloody kettle."

I went to check our fuses but everything seemed in order, then I noticed none of the houses in our street had lights on either.

Pointing this fact out to Mrs P didn't help because now the kettle was the cause of our neighbours' distress as well!

In fact, there were no lights at all in the whole area and I remember thinking, "surely a kettle cannot be capable of creating such mayhem?"

While Mrs P searched for candles, I was directed to phone our electricity supplier and inform them of the power cut.

I waited patiently as the minutes ticked by and then a machine told me, "I was in a queue but my call was important". Not sure if my call was important to the machine or the Electric Company, I continued to wait.

Suddenly the line crackled and a human voice said that they were aware of the fault in our area and were working on it. I relayed this information to Mrs P who in the meantime had placed our belated, lukewarm meal and the only candle she could find onto our dining table.

Sitting down, I remembered my visit to the library and what I learned, "arranging a late night meal for two, lit by a single candle," scores maximum points in the romance stakes!!!

I had done it, don't know how but I had succeeded, I had achieved my goal. This must put me on that pedestal alongside Romeo and Mr Darcy!!

I cleared my throat, paused for a few seconds and said in my most amorous of voices, "Well, this is so romantic."

Without a word, Mrs P fled from the room, "where are you going," I asked.

"To bed," came the brusque reply.

Now I knew that the whole objective of romance and the romantic mood was to make your partner **"conducive to, or suitable for lovemaking"** because I learned that in the library but somehow I got the feeling that with Mrs P saying, "she was off to bed" this did not necessarily mean that she was being conducive, so I stayed downstairs.

The next day I read in the local paper that the blackout was entirely due to thieves who had stolen some copper wire and switches from a sub-station.

It appeared that the total value of the scrap copper was under fifty quid but the damage done would run into tens of thousands. The theft had caused a surge in power and in some homes televisions, computers, washing machines and micro waves had all been rendered useless.

I said to myself, "they caused even more damage in our house by ruining my romantic gesture and you can't put a price on that."

I tried to point out to Mrs P that it wasn't the kettle's fault but all she said was, "I know whose fault it was, don't you worry!"

A month or so later, I tried again to evaluate just what had gone wrong and the best I came up with was that objects find it difficult to be romantic. Take a DVD player, it is tricky for it to be described as an amorous gift but if you buy one, then get your partner to settle down on the settee and watch "Gone with the Wind" or something similar then that's romantic.

I think it's the same with a kettle, buying it was correct but then I should have let her make two hot chocolates, settled her on the settee, in front of a roaring fire and watched "Kelly's Heroes"!

St. Valentine

Marble Co.

copper

Kelly's Heroes

Mr Pensioner

Chapter Four

March

"Brief Encounter"

"I am just a mole, in my field of dreams,
It's full of sheep but what that means,
With juicy, luscious worms, it teems,
It's mole heaven, or so it seems,
Until a catcher with traps and schemes,
Into my field, on quad, he screams."

Mrs Pensioner and I had taken up walking as a method of exercising while maintaining our aspiration of "spending time together" and on days when the weather permitted, we would cover over five miles.

During these excursions we would discuss world issues like the Financial Crisis, the troubles in Iraq or Afghanistan, even the possibility of another Royal Marriage but today a much more important topic had been on the agenda.

"What were we having for lunch?"

I had been given the usual selection list and was in the process of deciding; when we noticed that the number of molehills in a nearby field had increased dramatically.

Having observed only a few days previously that the field was (for the first time in our memory) occupied by a small number of the conical mounds, it now seemed an underground explosion had taken place and everywhere mini volcanoes were thrusting skywards. Having walked by this "mole free zone" almost every day for the previous 35 years, we could not let a momentous event like this take place without some debate.

Then as we surveyed the devastation, slowly absorbing the "earth shattering" spectacle while also valiantly trying to count the numerous piles of earth, the peace was broken by a raucous and very unexpected roar. Turning to face the direction from where the noise was emanating, we were just in time to see a strange figure burst over the brow of a small hill and continue his rapid charge towards us.

Like the Caped Crusader or a modern day John Wayne with his cloak trailing behind in the breeze, he quickly covered the short distance to reach us. This being the twenty first century however, our hero's familiar stallion had been replaced by a rather noisy quad bike and his cloak with a long waxed jacket. Bringing his "steed" to a halt he alighted and again, just like John Wayne he needed no introduction because there, emblazoned on the framework of his quad was the sign - "Mole Catcher".

Obviously we couldn't let an opportunity such as this pass without some discourse - after all how many occasions in life do you get to question a Mole Catcher and given our advancing years, the prospect of us ever having the chance again were slim.

So we took the easy option and our opening gambit was the same as is heard by every fisherman when approached by a passerby, -"Any luck yet?"

Unfortunately and possibly due to the racket still radiating from his four wheel stallion he didn't seem to hear us but then he either gave up trying to ignore us or more probably he realised that we weren't going anywhere until we had thoroughly interrogated him.

So cutting the engine he moved closer; obviously making the point that it was his vehicle's fault that we couldn't be heard and nothing whatsoever to do with the fact that he was working and did not want to be disturbed by two elderly citizens who had probably just been let out of the asylum for the day.

We tried again this time with our trusted, "Have you caught anything yet?" - You can tell by our line of questioning that we have a lot more experience with fishermen than mole catchers.

"One went through a trap as soon as I started," he reported.

Not wishing to show my ignorance in such matters and unable to ascertain if by "one going through a trap" meant it had been caught or not, continued with, "there's a bloody lot of them!"

"There's a lot of hills but they will have been caused by only 5 or 6 moles", he replied.

"If there are only 5 or 6 moles then they have been extremely busy because there were no hills here a few days ago," I countered.

"On average there about 3 moles to the acre," he stated.

"Well, we pass this field almost every day and never has there been mole hills on this scale before, so what's brought them?"

"Depends," came the extremely cagey reply, "what does the farmer use the field for?"

"Sheep," we answered in unison but I then went on to explain, "But only very recently because until then it was always used for silage or very occasionally cows."

"Well there's your answer, it is because of the sheep that the moles are here, they have attracted them," our informant retorted.

Silence briefly descended while we churned this statement very slowly, over and over.

Do moles really like sheep?

If they do - why?

Do sheep like moles, if so, how do they attract them?

If the moles are underground, how do they know that sheep are above the ground? These and numerous other questions were reeling round our minds but luckily our captured mole catcher came to the rescue.

He explained carefully that a sheep's excrement contained lots of nutrients which are extremely appetising to worms and other soil dwelling creatures. Therefore the numbers of these "earthly beings" multiplied considerably as they feasted on the delicious, organic banquet laid before them. In turn, the huge quantity of worms are very appealing to the moles who having determined that a new flock of sheep were in town, immediately took up residence in the aforesaid field.

Simples init?

So it seems but wait a minute, if the excrement attracts the worms and they are good for the soil, why does the farmer want to kill the moles?

It turned out that the moles can carry some diseases, which could infect the sheep that drop the excrement that attracts the worms.

Beaten, we gave up on this line of enquiry but taking advantage of our newly found font of mole knowledge, we decided to press our luck. So next we explained that in our youth, it was common to see dead moles hung on the fence enclosing a field. "Why and what was the reason for this practice," we asked.

Patiently we were told that this custom had two purposes. Firstly the Mole Catchers were paid according to the number of moles caught and this was a way of proving to the farmer just how much money the catcher was owed. Secondly, the moles were sometimes hung on fences which created the border between farms, it was hoped that this act would shame the adjoining farmer into making a contribution to the costs of the mole catcher.

By now it was becoming obvious that our captive was yearning for some solitude or at the very least for us to disappear. So not wishing to upset him further (because you never know when you might need the services of a first rate mole catcher) we took pity on him and bid farewell.

As we resumed our walk we saw him leap astride his "steed", which started with a roar and off he went – into the sunset – or so I thought but then the engine note changed, the machine leapt skywards and somersaulted. Whether or not it had struck a molehill or even a couple of molehills, I couldn't be sure but our new found friend was catapulted from the quad and both he and the machine hit the ground with a thud.

Mrs P and I went running to help our new chum who luckily was still able to speak. It took only seconds for him to agree with Mrs P that at least one leg had been broken, so I was dispatched to the farmhouse to persuade someone to phone for an ambulance.

I soon located the farmer who was resting with his feet up in the kitchen, enjoying a well earned cup of tea and I quickly explained the situation. He was very helpful and obviously extremely concerned, after all who was going to rid his field of moles now and as the accident took place on his land was he liable?

Unable to answer any of his questions, either legal or agricultural but with the cries of an injured mole catcher still ringing in my ears, I suggested a sequence of events in priority order exactly as I perceived them. These were;- phone for that bloody ambulance, then sort everything else after that.

The call was made and fifteen minutes later the ambulance arrived but because of the field's difficult terrain, the driver somewhat wisely decided against entering the field with his vehicle.

He made the point that if a quad bike had overturned, how could his ambulance cope with the tricky landscape?

So leaving the vehicle at the farm, the two ambulance men accompanied by the farmer and myself walked the short distance to where Mrs P was attending to the injured mole catcher.

After a detailed examination, the suspected broken leg was put in a splint and the patient was prepared for transportation. Then the two ambulance men began a bizarre debate which centred on the method by which the mole catcher should be moved. The conversation included using the services of an air ambulance and even the involvement of our local mountain rescue team. Remembering that even injured Premiership footballers are occasionally put in great danger by being carried from the field on a stretcher, I naively suggested that possibly the farmer and I could help by being conscripted as additional, emergency stretcher bearers.

My proposal prompted another discussion but after some deliberation, it was decided that provided we received some instruction on the art of lifting and carrying a stretcher, we could be of assistance.

So positioned at each corner, the four of us, with our feet shoulder width apart, stomach and back muscles locked, backs straight, hands firmly on the stretcher bars with palms facing upwards, weight evenly distributed on the balls of our feet, gently lifted on the count of three, the severely shocked patient.

Then very carefully we carried him towards the meticulously parked ambulance while Mrs P held his hand, wiped his forehead and kept him informed of the distance still to travel. With every step we took, the lead ambulance man issued new warnings regarding the slippery conditions and the precise location of the "deadly" molehills.

Incredibly we arrived at our destination without mishap, the stricken mole catcher was deftly placed inside the ambulance and five minutes later he was on his way to hospital.

I was hoping to be given the opportunity of recovering the quad but before I could offer my services, the farmer kindly volunteered to move and store it until the mole catcher recovered. Mrs P thought this was a brilliant solution so I somewhat disheartened, recommended to Mrs P that we should head home.

We were still discussing the unfortunate accident as we neared our house and Mrs P was wondering whether in some way we were responsible. Had we contributed to the mishap by questioning our latest acquaintance and would the accident still have occurred if we hadn't intercepted him?

Unfortunately I never had the chance to answer because there - right in the centre of our lawn and dominating our entire garden was the biggest molehill I had ever seen.

It was huge and how such a tiny creature as a mole could ever have built the structure in the short time while were out walking still baffles me.

Isn't life funny I said as we closed our front door, "we managed sixty odd years without needing or knowing a decent mole catcher and as soon as we find one, we need him but then we can't use him because he's on the sick!"

Mr Pensioner

Danger
Molehills

Mole Catcher

Chapter Five

April.

"Mobile Mayhem"

"It was the day of the game,
To miss it would be a shame,
But our Son needs a phone,
And the details are all known,
Arrangements had been made,
Then impeded by a raid,
With football sorely missed,
*Left feeling slightly *issed."*

It was Sunday, the first week of April and as on most Sundays, our son who is visually impaired was having dinner with us. We manage to call on him most days but on Sundays he visits us and we take the opportunity of catching up with all of his news of the week.

During the meal he casually told us that his mobile phone was broken and he was planning to buy a new model.

Apparently he had done some research and identified the necessary phone – a white i3GS.

He preferred a white one because he would be able to find it more easily than a dark colour and he also explained that the "S" in the i3GS was important to him because it signifies that the phone has "speech".

This meant the device was capable of "reading" his text messages and translating them into an audible, humanoid voice.

Immediately, Mrs P very kindly offered to buy one for his birthday. I wasn't exactly against this idea but as I pointed out, his birthday was still 6 months away and he needed the phone now.

This wasn't a problem to Mrs P, we would simply buy the phone now and tell him in 6 months time he had already received his gift. I reminded her that we had already bought him this year's birthday present twice previously. Firstly in the form of a short holiday which was closely followed by a large contribution towards his new bathroom.

In the scale of things I considered the cost of a new phone wouldn't be that damaging. However, I also thought that by the time his real birthday came along Mrs P would have forgotten all about the earlier gifts and would then insist on buying him yet another.

That amounted to four birthday presents in one year, at the very least!

I wondered if I could get away with a similar scheme but as Mrs P only seemed to suffer from selective memory loss when it involved the kids, probably not.

As I said though - a new phone they couldn't be that costly - could they?

So, as directed by Mrs P, I made a note of the make and model of the necessary phone with the intention of us buying one during our next shopping expedition.

That night while Mrs P was busy chatting to friends, I took the opportunity of discussing her latest charity event with Joe down at the club. I mentioned the type of phone required and through pursed lips Joe took a sharp intake of breath. You know, the sort of low whistling wheeze that garage mechanics must have spent their entire apprenticeships practising, so they can be absolutely perfect when you ask about the cost of any car repair.

"£400", I gasped, "surely not – you must have made a mistake Joe. Every child I see nowadays from the age of seven upwards seems to have one; they are always talking or that texting to one another. All of those parents can't be spending £400 on phones for their kids; some of the families near us have four children and there's one couple who have remarried and now they have a total of six children living with them. That's up to £2,400 on just supplying them with phones; you must have got it wrong, Joe".

Very carefully, Joe went on to explain that not all mobiles cost that much – some types were even given away, for free. Obviously, I then suggested that I would persuade Mrs P to buy one of the free ones but Joe informed me that I had to buy a contract to get a free one. "So how much are these contracts then," I enquired, while thinking at the same time, "this is easy; we buy a contract, get the free phone, then cancel the contract and keep the phone."

"£30 a month that's £360 a year but it's still better than paying £400," I said optimistically.

It turned out you have to keep the contract for a minimum of two years and if you cancel in that time the company take the money anyway.

"Bloody hell, Joe, I can't win", I exclaimed, and then continued with a query that I would regret saying for a very long time – a question that would cause me anguish every time I recollected the events that were about to unfold.

"Is there anything else I can do?"

Now I know that it doesn't sound an earth shattering enquiry but remember the phrase and judge it again later because I trace everything back to those fateful few words.

"Well", said Joe thoughtfully, "you could try the Internet, you may find one cheaper on there but I know definitely they are £400 in the shops".

Our discussion would have continued longer but just then Mrs P returned so we quickly changed the subject but not before Joe very kindly whispered in my ear, "I'll see if I can find a phone on the Internet for you."

Two days later Mrs P was doing her housework, vacuuming to be exact and I was valiantly trying to watch (and listen to) a television programme showing the build up to Manchester United's European Cup, quarter final. Very helpfully, I suggested she took her "noise machine" upstairs, where she could continue with her "good work" without any hindrance from me.

At least it's only the noise, I reflected and not like the old days when a vacuum cleaner could cause havoc with the television picture as well. Back then, as soon as the vacuum was switched on anywhere in the house, the entire TV screen would be covered with hundreds of white dancing dots making it very difficult to distinguish anything and certainly impossible to pick out a football.

It wasn't just our vacuum cleaner that caused a problem either because as soon as the lady next door started cleaning, **her** interference appeared on **our** television. I also believed she was a little bit mischievous because I never really could accept that she always had to start her cleaning at five past three on Cup Final day or whenever another important match was shown. I considered getting Mrs P to start her vacuuming at the same time as Gardener's World but somehow I never got round to it.

Later, suppressors became available and they lessened the effect from our "sound generating appliance" but I still suffered for a long time from our neighbour's machine, even after I had politely enlightened them to the existence of the miracle cure for interference.

I wonder what happened to the suppressers, are they now fitted "as standard" rather than an "optional extra"?

I suppose starter motors and windscreen wipers also began life on cars as optional extras but I was told recently that wheels are almost considered as optional extras on some of the more expensive German cars nowadays. With that in mind, perhaps suppressors will make a comeback after all. Maybe there's a wily old "Alan Sugar" who bought the world's stock, stored them and is waiting patiently for just that day.

Thankfully Mrs P accepted my kind-hearted proposal that she should resume her duties upstairs and after giving me a little look of disdain she disappeared, leaving me to watch the TV in peace. United's home tie was due to be played that night and I was really looking forward to it. It was a match I had no intention of missing because I had been a Manchester United fan for as long as I could remember. I am not sure when I first started to take an interest but I remember clearly the Busby Babes and of course the Munich disaster. I suppose, like millions of other people throughout Britain and the rest of the World, the tragedy cemented a fascination with the club. As a youngster, I would travel into Manchester and watch the matches from the terraces. Nowadays with the television coverage being so good and the exorbitant entrance fees, I much prefer to stay at home and watch.

So my entire evening was planned, Mrs P was going to visit her friend Big F but she would leave me sandwiches for half time and I already had some cans cooling in the fridge. This meant I could shout and swear as much as I wanted at the refereeing decisions without fear or rebuke and I wouldn't have to keep explaining the offside rule every few minutes.

The television programme was now showing United's Glory Days; there was Denis Law with his familiar goal salute, Best with his dribbling skills and Bobby was blasting them in with either foot, when it was all interrupted by a frantic knocking on our front door. Not wishing to miss a single detail, I waited in anticipation for Mrs P to respond to the thunderous knocking.

Unfortunately, due to the noise of her machine she was not aware of our visitor. So cursing under my breath about the inadequacy of the people who design vacuums and the short-comings of their products, I very reluctantly went to investigate. There, standing on our doorstep was Joe with, "good news" or so he said.

Then an amazing thing occurred; the deafening knocking had ceased and silence reigned, apart from the racket still emanating from Mrs P's favourite toy – that is - but guess what? She heard Joe whisper, "Good news" now how could she do that – it beats the laws of science. It was impossible for her to hear our front door being hammered but she managed to hear the faint murmurings of a human voice. I still can't understand how she achieved that feat but the vacuum was switched off, cast aside like an old broken doll and seconds later she was running down our stairs like an Olympic sprinter to greet Joe and hear his "good news".

He had located a phone for us, the exact model and in white!

He explained that white ones were as difficult to find as hen's teeth but he had done it!

Not only that but he had also negotiated the seller down to £300, saving us £100!

Joe was a hero, a regular John Wayne. Mrs P brought him a cup of tea and fussed over him – even offered him Jaffa Cakes, which he politely declined, settling for Rich Tea instead while he related the rest of his "good news".

It seems we were "very lucky" because the seller lived locally and he was only interested in cash. Apparently this meant we did not have to mess about with that Pay Mate thing and we could give him the money in person, when we collected the phone.

"Hang on a minute," I said interrupting Joe in mid flow, "Did you say that we have to collect the phone?"

"Well, yes," Joe replied.

There then followed a long dialogue of short phrases including;-

Where do we collect it?

Where is that?

How do we get there?

How will we know him?

How will he know us?

How do we know the phone will work?

All of which, without any hesitation whatsoever, Joe patiently answered while devouring the last of the Rich Tea in the process.

There were no apparent problems, Mrs P had the cash and Joe had thought of everything else, so the transaction would go like clockwork. We had the seller's name, address, mobile telephone number, an agreed meeting time and just to make absolutely sure; Joe even lent us his mobile should we need to contact the seller. Obviously, we needed to undergo an intensive training course on how to operate the phone but after forty minutes or so, Mrs P assured me that she had the hang of it.

It was then I realised the deal time had been arranged for 7pm that night!!!

As I received this bombshell, my enthusiasm began to wane because the timing gave me less than an hour in which to complete the transaction and drive home for the start of the match.

I considered the prospect carefully, it could be done – just - and if everything went perfectly I may even achieve the task with a few minutes to spare. In addition, I could also profit from earning lots of extra bonus points from Mrs P.

Balance that with being in the doghouse for the next three months, no contest - I had to go.

I persuaded Mrs P to set off early, my theory being that if the seller arrived before 7pm, then I would benefit from having more time in which to get home. Next I dug out my old A-Z of Manchester to find the road where the seller lived, which was also the agreed location for the transaction. It turned out there were three "XXXX" Roads in my A-Z but this was not a serious difficulty, we would simply ring the seller for clarification.

We tried several times during the next thirty minutes - all ending with the same result - no answer!

My surplus, safety-net time was dwindling but the setback was not yet considered a tragedy and as Mrs P was still intent on making the business deal, I proposed that we drive nearer to Manchester, park up and use Joe's phone to ring again. This we did but the outcome was the same, no reply.

By now I was beginning to get a bit twitchy and was just about to advise Mrs P that we should give up when the mobile borrowed from Joe rang or as I should say, it began to play, "I can't get no satisfaction" by the Rolling Stones. Mrs P began pressing buttons; apparently her crash course had only included instructions on how to make calls and not how to receive them. Eventually however she must have found the correct button and looking extremely pleased with herself, handed me the mobile. Putting it to my ear, I heard, "Hi der mon, you bin dingin me?"

After some difficulty and no thanks to the local knowledge of the resident at the other end of the phone, I managed to eliminate two of the "XXXX Roads," which left me with just the one possibility. Time was now at a premium, so I finished the call by telling our supplier that we were not far away and could be in "his road" within ten minutes.

With the help of the A-Z and Mrs P I soon found the nominated road and surprise, surprise there was even parking available.

Jumping out of the car, I walked up and down trying to find his house – number 58.

I found number 52 and I found number 64 but no 58 and where it should have been was just an empty space. Now a little concerned, I was breaking this news to Mrs P when Joe's mobile broke into song again. This time the correct button was depressed immediately and I was speaking to the "mobile man" once more.

I translated what he told me as, "He would be a little late because he had forgotten about a Doctor's appointment that he must attend". I informed him we were already parked in his road but his house was missing!

It turned out the address was his girlfriend's house and he couldn't remember the actual number. I told him, just a little sarcastically, not to worry because he was doing well to remember that he had a girlfriend, never mind where she lived. His only reply was to tell me to wait where I was and he would be with me soon.

As the minutes ticked by Mrs P and I became aware of a lot of people coming and going from one of the houses quite close by. Some arrived by car, a couple on bikes and a few on foot but all glanced up and down the road before they entered the house. I suggested that the occupiers probably had a huge flat screen TV and were holding a party for United fans but they did not want the neighbours to find out because they were City fans. So everyone invited to the party had been told to make sure they weren't seen entering the house.

Just then the Rolling Stones broke into song again and our forgetful Romeo told us his doctor's visit was over but he had to "bob" into Tesco to pick up some medicine. It "bobbed" into my mind that he could be "bobbing" into Tesco to pick up a mobile but I kept these feelings to myself.

With all hope of being home to see the start of the match now gone, I was evaluating the possibility of watching the second half when an old black BMW with blacked out widows came screaming down the road and screeched to a halt in front of us. The door swung open and out rolled an extremely tall bloke of Afro-Caribbean descent. He was dressed in black jeans with his head covered by one of those popular hooded jackets. I opened my car door to get out but before I could, he sat down in the road at my side, blocking any exit. My head and his head were almost at the same level even though he was on the tarmac. He began by telling me the phone was brand new, never been used and he was only selling it because he now had a Blackberry.

I remember thinking, if it had to be named after a fruit why not a banana? That was a much better name for a phone if only because of its shape. Why call it a Blackberry? Could it be considered racist?

What was the difference between a blackberry, a strawberry or even a gooseberry? Then I remembered Orange and Apple – all fruits and all connected to mobiles – should I take out the copy-rights of all of the fruits I could think of? I could then make a fortune selling the patent of a gooseberry or the exclusive rights to raspberry.

Meanwhile our supplier was still gushing about the merits of the white i3GS, when I noticed that the box was not printed with the i3GS logo. It had i3G but the essential "S" was missing.

This was easy to explain, the box was wrong, in his haste to meet us he had inadvertently picked up the wrong one but the phone was certainly the i3GS. It was a simple mistake; it could happen to anybody - couldn't it?

I thought I could sense Mrs P getting a little uncomfortable, what should we do?

Should we trust his word and give him the money?

His whole dress and manner suggested we shouldn't but how would we extricate ourselves from the deal?

Eventually Mrs P made the decision without any input from me whatsoever.

She thanked him and gave him the money, which he gratefully stuffed into his pocket without ever counting or checking. Then giving me the phone, he ran back to his car and I closed my door but just as I was fastening my seatbelt and he was driving off, a police car appeared from nowhere and squealed to a halt in front of him. Suddenly another police car materialised, this one stopping just in time to avoid hitting the mobile man's boot and then before I had time to react, a third pulled up alongside our car. Mrs P and I were ordered out while our car was searched and further down the road we could see the same happening to the man in the BMW. Next, Mrs P and I were separated and then pushed into the back of different police cars where we were each asked to give our story.

Two hours later and with our "alibis" checked, all three of us were allowed to leave. I am not sure who was the most embarrassed, us or the police. It seems they suspected that the venue for the "football party" was being used to deal drugs, so they were monitoring the house. When we arrived on the scene and the police saw money and a package change hands, they jumped to conclusions and decided to swoop.

With the sincere apologies of the police still buzzing in our ears, our drive home was a relatively quiet affair. I was picturing the possible headlines in our local paper – "Mr & Mrs Pensioner Captured in Major Drugs Bust" or "Mixed Up Drug Pensioners Arrested."

I had completely missed the football, even the fans had gone home but I learned from the radio that United went 3-0 up but then had a player sent off. They eventually won the match 3-2

but over the two legs the aggregate score was 4-4 and United were knocked out on the away goals rule - a bad night all round. Staying positive, I tried to console Mrs P by saying, "Some good may still come out of this - if the phone doesn't work, we can go to the police and obtain the mobile man's true address."
There was no reply.

A couple of days later our Son phoned to thank us for the mobile, it was exactly what he wanted and worked perfectly. I asked could there be any possibility of it being stolen? "No chance Dad," came the surprise reply, "I couldn't have registered it, if it had been stolen".
"No, there is nothing wrong or illegal with the phone, the previous owner probably upgraded to a Blackberry or something similar."

Later that night, I met Joe down at the club to return his phone and tell him about our "good news" but I purposely forgot to tell him about our exploits with the drug squad and the fact that I missed United's match.
I just thanked him for his help, saying that our Son was very pleased with the mobile.
"Don't mention it," said Joe, **"Is there is anything else I can do!!!"**

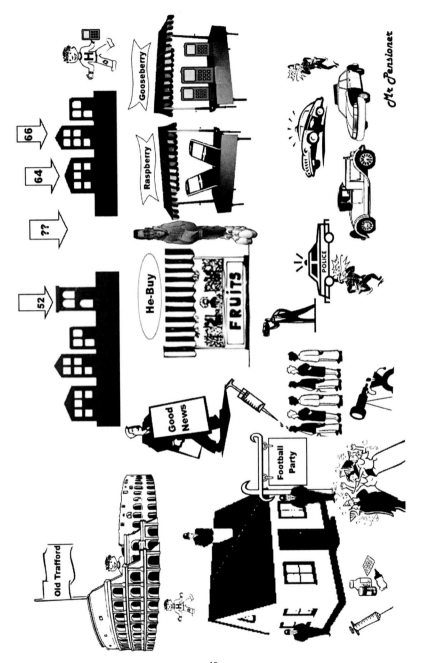

Chapter Six

May

"Fishy Story"

"Oh, what a beautiful day!"
The weather girl did say,
It seemed to start that way,
But could it really stay?
Such a perfect day - in May,
So, I began to pray,
But the answer came back - "Nay."

The TV weather girl had promised a beautiful day and for once, it seemed that she had got it right. The sun was shining brightly and already it was beginning to warm the early morning air.

It was because of the weather girl's optimistic prediction that I had decided to give Mrs Pensioner a very special and much needed treat - I was going to take her fishing with me.

It had been several years since Mrs Pensioner accompanied me on such a trip and although I couldn't remember the circumstances surrounding our previous fishing excursion, something deep in my memory told me the event hadn't been a complete success.

I did remember however, that for any subsequent outings she had always made excuses and stayed at home but on this occasion, she had agreed to accompany me because of our goal of "spending time together".

I had been planning this trip ever since I saw the Environmental Agency's advertisement informing people they needed to purchase a rod licence before they went fishing.

I ask you, £27 for a rod licence who would believe it!!!

When I was young, you could have bought the whole of "Brennan's Lodge" for £27 but with the intention of staying legal, I had grudgingly purchased the licence online.

Joe down at the club said it was easy, anybody could do it and after three or four attempts, it seems that I must have got it right because the postman delivered the expensive document two days ago.

I bought the maggots yesterday and learned that they are now sold by the pint!!

Mild, bitter and lager by the pint – yes, but maggots???

Strictly speaking, I suppose lager should be sold by the litre because it comes from that Common Market where bananas are straight and oranges are sold in kilos.

Thinking about it though, I suppose the tackle shop was breaking the law when they sold me a pint of maggots - should it have been half a litre?

Things were a lot simpler when old Billy Hargreaves would fill your maggot tin for thrupence.

Anyway, with everything packed and the costly paperwork in order, we set off for the Leeds/Liverpool canal.

Arriving without a hitch, I managed to park the car at a somewhat awkward angle on a soft grassy bank, expertly squeezing it between two large trees. I thought it would be quite safe, well out of the way of any passing tractors and the trees would keep it cool for our journey home.

Congratulating myself on my driving prowess, we walked the few hundred yards along the canal towpath to a suitable fishing spot. In no time at all I was fishing and Mrs Pensioner was completely engrossed in her latest romantic novel.

It was a beautiful day, birds singing, the sun beaming, so peaceful and relaxing – it was almost perfect.

A couple of hours passed very quickly and I had caught a few perch and half a dozen roach when suddenly I heard a loud splash and looking up, I saw a large animal swimming rapidly across the canal straight towards me.

It appeared to be about eighteen inches long and was fearlessly reducing the short distance between us. It had almost reached the bank below my feet and I was about to get up and run, (just possibly shouting a warning to Mrs Pensioner who was still blissfully unaware and totally absorbed in her book) when it turned 180 degrees and began to swim back, across the canal.

It was doing lengths! Just like the keep-fit swimmers in our local pool!

As it reached the opposite bank it turned again and began swimming back towards me but as it drew level with my float it disappeared beneath the murky water.

A semblance of poise and composure returned to me and I recollected the tales of someone starting a mink farm near this place in the fifties when fur coats were fashionable but most of the mink escaped and the farm eventually failed.

It occurred to me that this monster must be one of the descendants of the escapees.

I began to speculate what mink ate. Frogs probably or possibly fish, no not fish, I didn't think they could swim fast enough to catch them – the one I had seen was fast but surely not that quick.

Could they eat maggots?

I supposed they did, some anglers throw enough maggots in the canal to keep hundreds of mink well fed. Then I remembered I was baited with treble maggot; they could look very tempting to a hungry mink that had just finished his training session for the day and was now searching for his dinner.

That creature was the last thing I wanted to catch, so carefully pulling the line out of the water, I changed my bait to the smallest single maggot I could find.

Surely that tiny specimen would dramatically reduce the odds of catching the beast, I thought.

With no further sightings, tranquillity slowly returned but my relief was short lived because I suddenly realised that while I had been occupied by the creature, the sky had darkened and heavy rain was now imminent. I passed on my observations to Mrs Pensioner who suggested that we curtail our expedition immediately and I (given my recent encounter) willingly agreed.

Our decision however, was taken too late because the heavens suddenly opened and the rain fell in torrents. By the time we had packed away the fishing equipment and reached the car we were both absolutely drenched.

Cursing the abilities of the Weather Girl, I threw the tackle into the boot and was about to jump in the car when I noticed that the front tyre was completely flat.

Deciding to wait until the storm had passed before attempting to change the wheel, I took refuge in the car alongside Mrs Pensioner who for some reason seemed to be in a very bad mood. She sat without speaking and steam appeared to be emanating from every pore of her body. I think it was the effects of the hot sunshine followed by the cold rain that was causing the steam; it couldn't have been anything else - could it?

After almost an hour of complete silence inside the car the rain slackened a little, so I decided it was time for me to become a mechanic. Unfortunately the nice soft grassy area where I parked had been transformed into a muddy marshland and I needed to locate the jacking point on the underside of the car.

There was no alternative; I had to lie down in the mire to find it but luckily after a few attempts I was successful.

So with sludge now running freely down the inside of my shirt I had the jack in place.

Have you ever tried jacking three quarters of a ton of motor complete with a steaming senior citizen sat inside, out of a bog? I have; the more pressure that is applied to lift the car, the further the jack disappears into the quagmire.

I learned this lesson quite quickly and I now refer to it as my "First Principle of Jacking".

Remembering my school physics lessons with old Mr O'Malley, I decided to search the undergrowth for something "to spread the load".

Crawling about under hawthorn trees (sometimes on all fours) is another experience that is not recommended, especially at my age.

Eventually however, I found a discarded piece of fencing that did the trick. So with the wheel changed but shirt shredded, trousers torn and mud caked all over me, (as well as the car's seats), we set off home.

When we reached the safety of our drive, the silence was suddenly broken by Mrs Pensioner who simply said, "That is the very last time I ever go fishing with you".

I think it was the drop of water, which had collected on the end of her nose and was about to fall that brought the memories of our previous fishing expedition "flooding" back to me.

On that occasion I had caught a rather large bream and during the struggle I had hit Mrs Pensioner full in the face with it while it still wriggled furiously on my line. The shock of a cold, wet, slimy, bream weighing about 3lbs hitting her hard on the cheeks had knocked her off her stool and into the muddy canal water.

We returned home early that day as well I recalled but not wishing to make matters worse, I decided against mentioning it. Then as I unlocked the front door, the situation became really horrific because there on the floor amongst the post was another fishing licence!!

Recollecting that I had at least three or four attempts at buying the expensive licence, I began praying that the bloody Environmental Agency hadn't charged my credit card £27 for each try; otherwise I would have to learn how to use that "He Buy" thing to start selling my newly acquired licences on-line.

Mr Pensioner

57

Chapter Seven

June.

"Supermarket Sweep"

"I remember well the village shop,
Where the work was nonstop,
They sold it all, from Victory V's,
To furniture wax, made by Bees,
Supermarkets then came along,
Saying, " Old shops have got it wrong,"
But it seems they've a lot to learn,
If success, is what they yearn,
Business is not just taking profit,
It's helping society and being part of it,
From Mr Cross take some advice,
And don't just sell - at any price.
For in the public you must invest,
If you want to be - The Best."

In accordance with our "spending time together," I had agreed to accompany Mrs P on the necessary shopping excursions. Previously my job and the hours I worked had been enough of an excuse to make it totally impossible for me to attend any such trips, so my knowledge regarding the inside of supermarkets and their function was quite limited.

As a youngster though, I remember very clearly going into the local corner shop with a list of supplies for my Grandmother. That shop seemed to sell everything, Woodbines for my Granddad,

Dolly Blue for my Gran, Robin Starch for my Mother, Brasso for my Dad and Gob Stoppers for me.

In my memory there wasn't anything that the shop didn't sell, from firewood bundles to cakes, from Victory V's to clog irons but when I think back, the shop area was less than twenty foot square.

So how was it possible?

How could they cram everything that anybody could ever want into such a small area?

It wasn't just the stock that was packed in; they also had space for waiting customers to sit and enough room for the two shop owners to work.

Mr and Mrs Cross owned the shop and I cannot remember it ever being shut, apart from Sundays of course. I am not sure if they ever wanted to open on a Sunday but it would have proved impossible because the shop was next door to the Methodist Chapel. If however anyone in the village needed anything, a slight knock on the shop's back door was sufficient for them to be served by Mr Cross who would simply hand over the necessary goods and with a smile say, "Pay me tomorrow."

Of course all of the thankful customers did pay as soon as possible and usually spent more than they would normally have done, as a sort of "Thank You" to Mr Cross.

Apart from Sundays though, if I was awake the shop was open, so I can only assume that in those days I must have gone to bed very early and got up very late.

I remember going for a bottle of sterilised milk, so I could breakfast on cornflakes and in the middle of the night buying a bottle of "All Fours" cough medicine for my Gran. On both occasions the place was still open, so just when did Mr and Mrs Cross find time to sleep?

They sold cakes which Mrs Cross baked but when did she bake them? They sold fruit and vegetables which Mr Cross collected from the wholesalers but when did he have time?

It still remains a mystery to me.

Running the business must almost have been a twenty four hours a day operation and in later years the workload got even greater when Mr Cross began delivering groceries to some of the outlying farms, as well as to some of the locals who were either too old or too ill to shop for themselves.

There was also a seating area which consisted of four dark wood dining chairs, all placed side by side with their backs to the shop window, so that the occupants were all facing the counter. Three of the chairs were usually taken by the village's elder women who never seemed to buy anything but spent most of their days just chatting. Whenever a customer entered the three would take turns to say, "You can go first love, we're not in any hurry," and as a result the shop always seemed to have plenty of customers.

The fourth chair (nearest to the door) had several ancient magazines heaped on it but I don't think anybody ever read or looked at them and certainly no one ever moved them to sit down. This meant the magazines were always in the same order and perched precariously on the chair. That is until Old Tom Pritchard knocked them off one Saturday afternoon when he was drunk. He didn't just knock over the magazines though; all of the food tins suffered the same fate as well as a display of brushes, mops and buckets. Apparently Tom finished up with his face in a batch of freshly baked fairy cakes that Mrs Cross was about to take to Doctor Riley's for his birthday party.

It was rumoured the trouble started when Old Tom having spent Friday night and most of Saturday in the Bay Horse pub decided to buy a packet of Capstan on his way home. In the shop he saw Mrs Williams (one of the three wise women who normally occupied the chairs) and thought he would steal a kiss. Mrs Williams, a widow for twenty years thought differently and sent Old Tom flying with a haymaker that Joe Louis would have been proud of.

The resulting chaos was the main topic of conversation for the three wise women and most of the customers during the next five weeks, well certainly until young Jenny Grey ran off with Percy Dutton to get married.

In effect the shop was the heart of village society, a mixture of community centre, meeting place, counselling clinic and information centre.

It was the Village focal point where help and advice were freely given, as well as being the original convenience store – a place to buy anything and everything.

When I was six we moved from the village to the edge of a small mill town and this brought the delights of a High Street with its wide variety of shops within my range. There was even a toy shop; I couldn't get over it – a whole shop selling toys – nothing else just toys. It had everything, Meccano, model aeroplanes, toy soldiers, jigsaws, as well as Dinky and Corgi models. Of course it sold dolls and prams as well but they were for girls – urhg – and who wanted to play with their things?

There was also the Tripe Shop - now who would believe that today, a whole shop selling nothing else but tripe!

I never touched the stuff but my Dad loved it and occasionally I was sent to buy his favourite sort - Honeycomb Tripe. I remember once, riding home with two pounds of the substance in a thin plastic bag that I carried on the handlebars of my new bike.

To reach home I had to go down Castle Hill, which was the steepest in the area and brilliant for going down but murder for riding up. During the descent it was possible to pick up a considerable speed but at the bottom there was a tight left hand bend to negotiate. This hill was the scene of numerous accidents, one I remember involved Aspinall's coal lorry, it failed to take the bend, turned onto its side and slid into Jimmy Jones's pigeon coop, completely demolishing it. There was feathers and coal everywhere. Obviously the entire neighbourhood (being a caring community) came out to help sweep up the mess but they did seem more interested in moving the coal to safety rather than the wellbeing of Jimmy's pigeons. The driver was taken to the Black Bull pub for a few drinks to help him recover from his ordeal while the good people of the area "cleaned up".

Quite a number of families had pigeon pie in front of a roaring fire that night and funnily enough the Black Bull was renamed the Three Pigeons but that was many years later.

Anyway, travelling at high speed I reached the bottom of the hill and turned the handlebars to navigate the dangerous bend. Unfortunately the thin, white plastic bag dangling from my handlebars and holding the delicacy which was the Honeycomb tripe got caught in the spokes of the bike's front wheel. The bag was shredded and so was the tripe - in tiny particles it flew from the wheel splattering my school pants and embedding in my best "Mrs Cross's hand-knitted woollen jumper".

I managed to salvage some of the tripe, not much but enough I thought to lessen the blow when I arrived home. The problem was there wasn't enough of the plastic bag left intact to put it in, so with no other option, I decided to carry it home "loose" in my pants pocket!

During the first few months following my retirement, I had been educated in the ways of the supermarket and had learned enough to be trusted to check on the latest price of a bottle of Rioja or the latest offers on beer.

I soon realised the supermarkets had copied Mr and Mrs Cross's notion of the village shop by trying to sell everything and anything. In fact they had even tried to take the concept further by also providing fuel, insurance and banking facilities. Although to be fair, Mr Cross had already instigated the banking facility when he introduced his Christmas savings club and when I think about it, he also provided fuel. Ok, he didn't sell petrol - there was no need because few people owned a car but he did sell bundles of firewood and paraffin for their stoves, so yes, he provided fuel as well.

Nowadays some supermarkets have begun delivering to their customers' homes - another innovation of Mr Cross. It seems to me that he was the creator of the modern supermarket, the John Logie Baird of shopping and what's more he was from my village!

Ah! but I hear you saying that he didn't have a clothes section like Tesco or Asda. Well maybe not but he did supply clothes because every new baby born in the village was presented with a matinee coat - hand knitted by Mrs Cross. Her goodwill, free sample idea resulted in a constant stream of orders for all types of pullovers and cardigans which she sold at a handsome profit.

It seems to me, the supermarkets have still a lot to learn from the Cross's.

Maybe they will introduce a seating area where people can chat on a rainy day or dare I say it, provide some personal service!

Maybe even train someone who can recall a customer from their last visit or remember that they prefer butter to Stork!

Or even someone who says, "Hello Mr P how are you today?" but I suppose that is asking a bit too much!

Having undertaken training myself at the hands of Mrs P, I had developed from just being capable of scrutinising the price of beer. I had been promoted and was now qualified enough to place some of our purchases onto the checkout belt. Obviously I am still not considered experienced enough to put them all on or at the other side of the till, take anything off and position any in our trolley but who knows in a few more years, after I have completed my apprenticeship?

However my recent upgrade to Assistant Loader of Checkout Belt was enough of a promotion for the time being and basking in the glory of the extra responsibility, I thought I was fast becoming a great help to Mrs P.

Until she informed me that my inclusion on these fascinating excursions cost us up to twenty pounds a trip extra. According to her, I always persuaded her to buy something that she wouldn't have bought, if she had been alone.

I heard her discussing this notion with Mrs Regan who lives at number 56 and both were in agreement that partners accompanying the shopper adds to the total spend of the weekly shop.

Personally, I can't see this being true but if it were, the supermarket owners would only have to offer a £5 discount to all women who did their shopping accompanied by their partner. The supermarkets would then make a fortune; turnover would be up, the suppliers would be happy because they were supplying more, the producers would be happy because they had to produce extra and the housewives would be happy because of the £5 discount. What's more, because the supermarkets would then buy in greater bulk they could negotiate lower prices with the suppliers. These could then be passed on to us, the consumers and the price of everything would fall, making inflation a thing of the past.

All it needed now was to prove Mrs P's assumption to be correct and I would be feted as the man who beat inflation, (a problem the world's politicians have been trying to solve since Roman times). Then I could say, "Margaret Thatcher eat your heart out," after all she was a shopkeeper most of her life whereas I have only been visiting supermarkets for a few months.

While visualising my award of the business equivalent of the Nobel Peace Prize, I helped Mrs P to complete the successful purchase of our weekly supplies by pushing the fully loaded trolley to our car, where we both began loading our provisions into the boot. Suddenly I noticed that another car, parked directly opposite had started to reverse from its bay straight towards us. "No worries," I thought, "They can see us and there's plenty of room for them to manoeuvre or stop."

Unfortunately the car didn't stop; it hit our trolley, which was then pushed into Mrs P who at the time was placing several of Warburton's finest loaves into our car boot.

She was trapped; her knees were hard against our car bumper, the trolley was cutting into the backs of her legs and the offending car was still pushing into the trolley.

To make matters worse, at the time of the impact Mrs P was bent over with her head in our car boot and it was now impossible for her to stand up. This was due to the extreme pressure on her legs as well as the angular shape of the trolley, which was forcing her body downwards, deeper into our boot. Several other shoppers, having seen the incident began shouting. I ran to the car and banged on the side window in an attempt to alert and stop the aberrant driver (a woman) from reversing further. I noticed she was looking forwards through her windscreen, even though the car she was controlling was still trying to move backwards. Thankfully, she stopped but still unaware of what the commotion was about, she got out of her car to see what was happening. At this point, I and a couple of other people told her quite unceremoniously to get back in and move her car forwards.

With Mrs P released, the store manager and a few of his colleagues including the Health and Safety officer arrived at the scene. They took Mrs P, the deviant driver and a couple of witnesses into the store to assess the injuries and to take statements.

Meanwhile I was ordered to finish the transfer of our shopping from the trolley and while doing so, I took the opportunity of inspecting our car for signs of damage.

I learned later that the hapless driver who caused the accident said in her statement that she was suffering from a very stiff neck, which made it impossible for her to turn her head. Obviously she was unable to see anything, except what was straight ahead. The store manager strongly advised her against driving until her condition improved, which it must have done almost immediately because I saw her driving off just before I entered the store to look for Mrs P.

It turned out that Mrs P was lucky; she didn't require hospital treatment, only suffering some small cuts and severe bruising to both legs.

I told her she was a hero for preventing any damage to our bumper with her selfless act of cushioning the impact between the trolley and our car.

Later, I was allowed to drive us both home and I only received two minor reprimands during the whole journey. However, a third and very severe one was imparted, when it was found that our recently purchased ice cream had completely melted.

Obviously Mrs P felt that this mishap was entirely my fault but as I pointed out, it could never have occurred in Mr Cross's time. Back then we employed "Just in Time" principles and reduced the transfer time by eating the ice cream as soon as we left the shop!

Aspinall's Coal Merchant

Tripe

Mr Pensioner

Chapter Eight

July.

"Summer Holiday"

"It wasn't a race,
But one hell of a chase,
And now, so very tired,
Is a man, who has retired,
But moving like a rocket,
He tries to save that locket!"

It was mid-July and Mrs Pensioner and I were on holiday.

After enduring weeks of wind and rain at home, we had promised ourselves two weeks in the sun, so here we were in Spain's Andalusia region.

Is there a better place in which to relax, unwind and take it easy?

If there is, then we haven't found it and so far the holiday was proving to be everything the brochure had promised – Sun, Sea, Sand and Sangria.

Unfortunately however our days spent lazing in the sun were beginning to take their toll and an atmosphere of listless lethargy had descended upon us.

I had nothing left to read, other than a local guidebook, which also contained what were described inside as, "useful everyday Spanish phrases". The book had been my faithful companion during the last five days and while it only contained 24 pages, it had proved invaluable. Not for the information it contained of course but as the ultimate deterrent against bored and boring fellow holidaymakers. I had discovered that whenever I was approached by any irritating tourist, I could simply lower my head into the dependable book and they would change course to find some other person to annoy.

Obviously I had read the book from cover to cover numerous times but the size made it so handy that it could be carried quite easily – even in shorts. Amongst the "useful" phrases I learned were, "Me puede recomendar una canguro de confianza?" which basically means, "Can you recommend a reliable babysitter?" an essential expression that every pensioner needs to know.

As I said previously though, Mrs Pensioner and I were feeling very lacklustre, so in an effort to break the monotony and inject some fizz back into our dreamy, languid state, we decided to visit Fuengirola.

The town was described as, "one of the liveliest seaside resorts that form part of the Costa del Sol" in my precious guidebook and just how accurate, prophetic and useful this book was, we were about to discover.

We were strolling extremely slowly along the promenade of Fuengirola and our excuse for the leisurely pace was "we were absorbing the atmosphere."

In reality we were both incredibly hot because as is normal for this part of the world during July, it was a beautiful day. The sun was beating down and a faint breeze was wafting baking hot air towards the sea. Even bending down to tie a shoelace, meant sweat was immediately discharged from every pore of the body - it was that kind of day. Not exactly what you would describe as bracing and certainly not by Blackpool standards but without any exaggeration at all, you could certainly say it was, "fairly warm".

It was so much better than the weather back home though - provided of course that the countless reports relayed to us by our fellow holidaymakers were true. Apparently in the whole of

England it had not stopped raining for the last two weeks and the winds were whipping up to gale force but worse was still to come with very severe storms being forecast for the next seven days.

Now we had only been in Spain for a week and prior to our departure it had rained but no more than is normal for the height of an English summer. So even though Mrs Pensioner and I felt that the climatic conditions being experienced in the Motherland and relayed to us with such enthusiasm were greatly exaggerated, we were still feeling pretty pleased with ourselves for choosing the "right fortnight" for our holiday and for missing the "monsoons" back home.

Helping to reinforce the sense of our good fortune, we had un-wittingly sauntered passed several strategically placed columns on top of which sat huge clocks, all displaying an accurate time and current temperature in 3 foot high digits. Thirty seven degrees Centigrade and still the hottest part of the day to come - now that is warm for someone from Lancashire!

Mrs Pensioner had suggested a cooling drink and I obviously thought it was a tremendous idea. So I recommended a bar which I had made a mental note of earlier in the day because of its "All-Day-Happy-Hour" slogan. Luckily for me it was only a few yards away - but unluckily for me - I never got to that bar because a man suddenly appeared from the ambling crowd and seemingly struck Mrs Pensioner around the throat. Gasping and grabbing her neck she screamed, "He's got my locket, he's stole my locket!" Realising the enormity of the situation "almost" immediately, I turned and gave chase, leaving a shrieking Mrs Pensioner rooted to the spot.

"Not the locket, anything but the locket," my brain yelled. It wasn't the cost of it or that it was gold or that I had bought it for Mrs Pensioner nearly forty years ago. It was the memories that the locket held and the fact that it had become the symbol of our lives. Mrs Pensioner had worn it every single day since Christmas 1973 and even though much better and more expensive pieces of jewellery had been added to her collection, she always chose to wear the locket. At every subsequent event in our lives – weddings, christenings, birthdays, even funerals, the locket had been present, a constant in an ever changing world; the ultimate representation of our existence together.

Inside were fading photos of the kids, taken when they were three or four. On the outside were a couple of innocuous dents - bite marks made by our daughter when she was teething. So this man had not just stolen a gold locket, he had taken what was possibly Mrs Pensioner's most treasured possession - an emblematic talisman that retained her memories.

By the time I had turned and gathered some momentum the thief was a good thirty yards in front of me. I began to shout – as loud as I possibly could, "Stop him, he's a thief". The promenade was packed with people, surely someone would stop him. Then he turned right, into a street that went directly away from the sea. There were less people but still enough to stop him. I yelled again, "Call the police" and "Stop the thief." I even remembered the very useful guidebook that I had spent the previous five days studying. So I shouted in my best Spanish, "llame la policia" and "el ladrón" but again no one intervened. People watched, oh yes plenty of people turned and watched but no one helped.

He went right again, now we were running parallel to the seafront and we had covered well over a hundred yards.

One hundred yards! - I had sprinted a hundred yards! – Not jogged or trotted but sprinted!

Who would believe it!

I hadn't run so fast, for so far, in the last thirty-odd years. Not since I gave up football training and what's more I can't remember breathing. Shouting yes, I had had done a lot of shouting but out of breath? - Never!

When I think back over the events of that day, which I must confess I have done many times, I believe it was the first hundred yards that saved me because in my mind I really do believe that I cut down the distance between us. Not by much but by about five yards and enough I think to unsettle the thief.

The robber continued running along the street parallel to the sea but now he kept looking back, staring at me.

Was it because he couldn't believe I was still running or was he getting tired?

Two hundred yards had come and gone and for the first time doubts were beginning to enter my head. The pace had dropped markedly and I was definitely breathing now, big gulps of searing hot air were being taken at more than regular healthy intervals and my legs had developed a sort of jelly quality.

He turned left up a slight hill, I could feel it now, my lungs were bursting and I was beginning to accept the fact that I probably couldn't catch him.

Nevertheless I decided that I was going to keep running for as long as I could see him. Sweat was pouring off me, stinging my eyes, my legs were heavy and my throat was beginning to hurt. Whether it was the running or the shouting I don't know but my mouth was so dry I was having difficulty swallowing.

The three hundred yard mark had been passed and I knew I couldn't keep going much longer but I was still only about twenty to twenty five yards behind him.

Then he turned left again and as he went round the corner of the buildings I lost sight of him. When I turned the same corner, I expected to see him just ahead but the street was empty, completely devoid of people.

I had lost him and feelings of utter despair enveloped me but he couldn't have gone far, he had been just in front of me. People can't just disappear he must be somewhere, so I stopped a short distance into the street and listened.

On my right was a row of terraced houses which fronted directly into the road and continued for as far as I could see, there was nowhere for him to hide there. On my left was a line of parked cars and a very high wall, surely he couldn't have climbed that barrier in such a short time? He must have gone into one of the houses but anyone disappearing into a house so quickly must make some noise, so I listened more intently.

There was nothing, nothing at all, just silence and the gloom of despondency returned.

I had lost him, I couldn't believe it - not in these circumstances - I had resigned myself to the fact that I couldn't catch him but to lose him, especially when I was still so close.

Then as I turned to retrace my steps I saw the tip of a foot underneath one of the parked cars.

I had found him; it had to be him, anyone working on the car would be facing upwards, looking up at the vehicle, not face down to the tarmac, it was him!

Instantly my tiredness disappeared and I crept silently and carefully towards the "foot".

Bending down I could see an ankle, so reaching under the car I closed on it with both hands. Then gripping as firmly as possible, I pulled with all of my strength. Out slid the thief and now it was his turn to yell. Letting go of his ankle, I dropped on to him using all of my weight to hold him down.

For a few seconds I was on top and I had him but as he squirmed frantically, I realised for the first time that he was bigger, stronger and a hell of a lot younger than me.

During the chase I was aware that he was younger but I hadn't given it a thought until now and I certainly hadn't considered what would be the consequences of catching him.

As we rolled about in the road the tables were beginning to turn and I was tiring rapidly, even my arms were aching now as I tried to hold him.

A crowd had gathered at the end of the street, drawn by my previous shouts and the sight of two men wrestling on the tarmac. Trying again I roared, "Help me, he's a thief" but the result was the same, nobody moved. Then with more good luck than skill I managed to get my opponent into a headlock, a hold I had seen perfected by Mick McManus all those years ago on black and white TV. Maybe I hadn't been wasting my time watching the wrestling when I should have been doing something more productive.

Could it be in the great scheme of things, it had been ordained that I had to watch and learn - just for this occasion? If so, I wish the planned occasion had happened sooner, when I was younger, fitter and stronger.

Whenever Mick was in trouble I recalled, he would resort to the headlock and hold onto his opponent until the bell rang to save him.

Could I do the same? Probably not, who the hell would ring the bell anyway?

As I held the headlock I became aware of a car moving very slowly towards us but it was impossible for it to pass because we were using the space normally allocated to cars for our fight.

Looking up but still maintaining Mick's favourite hold, I could also see the car windows were down and a man and woman were inside. "Probably a Spanish husband and wife out shopping," I remember thinking but with one last desperate shout, I repeated my cry for help in English and my best guidebook Spanish.

This time there was a response and leaving the car the couple walked slowly and very calmly towards us.

From my tarmac position I could see the man was not only considerably bigger than me, he was also considerably bigger than the robber.

Taking hold, "my saviour" dragged us both from the road and up against the wall, where his "wife" joined us. She stood directly in front of me and seemed more than a little hostile and undeniably aggressive. Could it be that our fight had upset their shopping plans, had she been promised a new dress and we had quite literally blocked their path? I definitely didn't wish to upset her, not a woman of her proportions, if she said it was Christmas Day then it was Christmas Day – even in this heat.

She reminded me of the Russian shot putters Tamara and Irina Press but I knew she couldn't be either of them because she was much too young. The Press sisters were World Champions in the early sixties and this woman was still only in her thirties.

Could she have been their daughter, I thought? Probably not, I conceded, remembering the gender rumours of the time.

My "saviour" was obviously asking what was going on but my newly acquired Spanish words had almost run out, so I blurted out my story in English about my opponent being a thief.

Then it was the thief's turn to explain and I am sure he said he had done nothing wrong, because the word "nada" (nothing) kept cropping up in his version. I also got the impression he was saying that I had just attacked him in the street.

Then my saviour produced a police badge and "Mrs Christmas" produced a mobile into which she was bellowing instructions. Just how lucky could I get, I had stumbled into two plain clothes police officers.

The thief was searched but to my dismay, no locket was found. Then, obviously having been summoned by "Mrs Christmas" the cavalry arrived with blue lights flashing and sirens blaring. Even the Spanish Police would not dare to cross her by turning up late and to ensure that she would have no cause for complaint, not one but two official police vehicles had been dispatched. Each car was complete with two "Policia Local" and even better, one of them could speak English fluently.

I was repeating my story when Mrs Pensioner arrived on the scene accompanied by several bystanders who had witnessed the event and luckily for me, they identified the thief.

The small crowd of spectators had now grown considerably and people were leaving the sanctuary of their homes (even though it was still siesta time) to see what was going on. A comfortable chair and cool drinks were produced for Mrs Pensioner but there was none for me because now I had to show the police the route of the chase.

So while Mrs P was being pampered and plied with drinks, two policemen escorted me all the way back to the promenade to search for the missing locket. We looked under cars, in gutters and flower beds but all in vain. Then when all hope seemed lost, one of the policemen got a call to tell us the locket had been found underneath one of the parked cars at the location of the "fight".

Thank goodness!!

Now I could collect Mrs P and go for what I thought was a very well deserved drink!

As I arrived back at the fight site however, it was plain that the audience had multiplied significantly. Kids were re-enacting the recent events by chasing one another, more kids were slightly behind and pretending to be the police by making "neeh-naah" sounds. There was a constant stream of witnesses, all wanting to say that they had seen "The Chase" and all wanting to give their story to the police. "Where were they when I needed them?" I thought. Two "Lucky-Lucky men" were taking full advantage of the throng by doing a steady trade in DVD's and watches. A woman of Chinese origin was trying to sell novelty toys but I don't think she was doing much business. An accordion player who seemed to be of East European extraction was playing an unrecognisable tune and a small, skinny, bespectacled bloke was asking some of the spectators to take photos of him as he posed bizarrely and extremely close to Mrs Christmas. The top of his balding head barely reached past her waist line and one of her enormous legs probably weighed more than his total body weight. It was a risk that I would not have taken under any circumstances but her stern facial expression seemed to have softened slightly and there was even a hint of a smile.

Pushing my way through the multitude, I was bundled together with a suitably refreshed Mrs Pensioner into one of the police cars. Through the car's open window I got what turned out to be my last ever glimpse of Mrs Christmas and I swear she was beaming from ear to ear at the peculiar looking man who was still posing for photos but now with his arm tightly wrapped around her.

The thief was handcuffed into the back of the other police car and leaving the mini-fiesta behind we all proceeded to the police station, with me still feeling parched and desperate for any sort of a drink.

Immediately on arrival Mrs P and I were taken to an interview room where we were told that before any further progress could be made, we had to undergo a hospital examination. Our protests fell on deaf ears and the lines of blood trickling from my scraped knees and down my legs were repeatedly pointed to.

It was clear that this was one argument we weren't going to win, so reluctantly we capitulated. Then we learned that the hospital was at the other side of Fuengirola and to make matters worse, we had to make our own way there. Mrs P and I were consulting maps when we got (not for the first time that day) a lucky break because the policeman who could speak English took pity on us and offered a lift in his squad car.

The drive through the busy back streets of Fuengirola to the hospital was relatively uneventful; after all you can't see that much through the blacked-out, rear passenger windows of a

Spanish police car. However, looking through our driver's windscreen we noted the ease with which "our" police car managed to join the oncoming traffic at every road intersection. Other drivers would bring their cars screeching to a halt then smiling broadly they would wave our car through. I can only believe that we encountered the most courteous and polite drivers in the whole of Spain during that journey.

It was thanks to those good mannered citizens that we completed our journey in half of the time it would normally have taken. Parking wasn't a problem for us either because the police car was simply left in a "positively no waiting area", after all who was going to risk towing away a police car.

So flanked by the helpful policemen, we entered the raucous, overflowing hospital waiting room where an immediate silence prevailed and all eyes turned on us. Obviously everyone in the room thought we were hardened criminals who had been forcibly apprehended by their Guardian Law Enforcers. If the sudden appearance of two foreigners under armed guard weren't enough, a quick check on my torn, sweat-soaked, filthy t-shirt and bloodied legs soon convinced everyone in the room that they could sleep soundly in their beds following our apparent capture.

Gradually, whispers began to return to the waiting area but all of the murmurings were concerning us and not their own conditions, (a first I think for any hospital waiting area). Then suddenly the doors burst open and the thief was frogmarched in; both hands were handcuffed behind him and two policemen were unceremoniously pushing him through the crowd. A gasp left the throat of every patient and carer; this was one hospital visit they wouldn't forget in hurry and something they could talk about in their local café for the next few days.

For a brief moment my eyes and the thief's met, it was just like a scene from a spaghetti western when Clint Eastwood and the baddie stare out one another before the big gunfight. The air was crackling with electricity and the "vibes" were detected by everyone present, so in anticipation of a thrilling climax, silence descended once again. Everybody waited for the finale but to the utter disappointment of the whole audience, my "guard" broke the spell by physically moving a Spanish patient and telling me to sit down in the now vacant seat. Then the thief's guards pushed him through another door and the whispers began to rise again.

Without any further sightings of our assailant, we were examined, given our official fitness certificates and returned to the police station.

We were then informed that an official translator was required to take our statements but none would be available until the following day. Secretly, I was very thankful because it was apparent that making a statement in Spain could easily take a couple of hours and I had still not received the promised cooling drink. So with the sun setting, we agreed to return "mañana" and I dragged Mrs P into the nearest bar.

Suitably cleaned and rehydrated, we returned the next day but as our statements were being taken; the office door burst open and in strode a very imposing character. I could tell he was important because both of the policemen interviewing us jumped to their feet and saluted. Through our translator we learned that he was the "Chief of Police" and he had come specially to see "the old man who had captured the thief".

"It's incredible, how could you catch him when you are so very old?" he asked via the interpreter.

Thinking I should be doing something more practical with my last days on earth, like ordering my coffin, it was taking me some time to come up with a suitable answer and before I could, he went on to add but this time in English, "me no him can caught".

There followed a very long pause when nothing was said by anybody. I think the silence was caused by the fact that our translator was having some difficulty interpreting that phrase. So before anybody reacted, the Chief pointed at our two interviewers and continued with, "them two, no use, no can caught nobody".

The ashen faces of the interviewers told me they could speak English just as well, if not better than the Police Chief and they knew exactly what was being implied.

Luckily, the translator averted the tricky situation from developing further by saying that the Police Chief and the interviewers were a bit younger than me and thought I had done extremely well to catch the thief.

The Police Chief then very kindly offered me a job on the force but I graciously declined, "on age grounds". He then shook my hand, stepped back and saluted before striding out.

Our interviewers made several gestures towards the door through which the Chief had just exited and continued speaking to one another in phrases of only two or three words (none of which were translated to us) for the next few minutes.

With our interview complete, we learned that the thief was a 19 year old Moroccan who was suspected of being responsible for a number of similar thefts in the area.

In these previous cases the thief had always evaded capture despite the best efforts of the police but now his trial would take place the following day at 10-00 am in Fuengirola Court and it would only take a few minutes ....

So with the guidebook being proved accurate in its description of Fuengirola and both mine and Mrs P's lethargy totally eradicated, we travelled again to the "lively resort" for a third consecutive day.

Arriving very early, we found the courthouse without any difficulty and settled into the waiting area. Handcuffed prisoners with gun carrying guards on either side were regularly transported from the basement, through the waiting area, into the court and back again. Some left minus the handcuffs but one unlucky individual made the same journey four times but always returned in handcuffs.

At one point a scuffle broke out when an old woman attacked one of the prisoners while he was being escorted through the waiting area. I had never seen a handbag wielded with such accuracy or ferocity before; I am sure it must have contained a house brick and how she managed to land so many blows in such a short time is a mystery? Even then, as she was hauled away and with her handbag out of range, she landed a devastating kick with her left foot into the hapless victim's nether regions, leaving him crumpled on the floor and gasping for air. Mrs P held the opinion that the guards holding the prisoner had positioned him with pin point precision to enable the blow to strike home with such a destructive effect. I wasn't sure about that but I was positive that Bobby Charlton at the height of his career had never kicked a football so hard.

Ten o'clock came and went, so did eleven o'clock and so did 12 o'clock. Mrs P was becoming agitated and because she now considered me fluent in Spanish; (thanks to my guidebook) I was dispatched to enquire, "What was happening."

Unfortunately even my newly acquired Spanish language made no impression and I was brusquely told to sit down by a court official.

At 12-30 pm a translator appeared and told us that it was our turn now and if the prisoner pleaded guilty, it would only take a few minutes………………

I remember thinking, I am sure I have heard that before.

Unfortunately the prisoner did not plead guilty; the case was referred to the High Court and we had to wait a further two hours while another forest of paperwork was drafted, printed and certified. The latest documents stated that the new trial was set for Court Number 6 at Malaga's "City of Justice" in November and our translator told us that, "we did not have to be present at the trial but it would be better if we were there".

Mrs Pensioner was of the opinion that we should attend but I was not convinced – possibly due to the costs involved, however we decided to call a truce for the time being and give the matter more thought once we were back in Blighty.

Back home we showed the paperwork to a very accomplished Spanish speaking friend who is Spanish by birth. After studying it for some time, he told us that we had to attend, otherwise our names would be added to the Police Wanted List and we could be fined up to 5,000 Euros each.

Could anything have been lost in the translation I thought? The new interpretation definitely varied from the original version. Firstly we were told we did not have to be there, then only a few days later, Interpol could be involved and we could end up paying a massive fine. Bibles had been translated from one language to another, hundreds of times over the last 2,000 years; our translations were only 5 days apart and only involved 2 languages.

With so much variation in just a few days, could it be that Jesus was really a baddie and the devil was right all along?

I thought the thief was the sinner and we were the sinned against but the way things were going we could end up in prison and the thief receive compensation for me attacking him.

The decision however had been made for us, 10,000 Euros against a few hundred pounds – no contest – we were going back!

So we made Mr Easyjet that little bit richer and bought two return tickets to Malaga.

Later that same evening we were relaxing at home, Mrs P was busy knitting while I sipped a beer and mulled over the recent events.

I wasn't relishing the idea of returning to Spain for the trial in November but I have to admit, I was feeling fairly pleased with myself for catching the thief and for recovering the precious locket.

My feelings of elation however, were completely destroyed in one sentence by Mrs P who simply said, "don't get upset about it love, I know you would have caught him a lot sooner, if it hadn't been such a hot day."

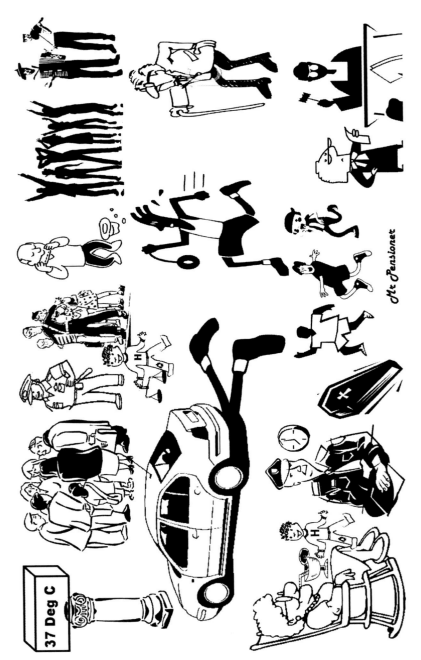

Mr Pensioner

37 Deg C

Chapter Nine

August.

"Happy Camp"

"Invited for a few days break,
To go on holiday by the lake,
But it was, just one big fake,
All implemented by a snake,
While their money he did take,
Their spirit he could never break."

Mrs P and I had been invited to spend a few days in the Lake District and as everyone knows, it is a beautiful location.

As well as being the largest National Park in England, the area also includes England's highest mountain in Scafell Pike, the deepest lake with Wastwater and the largest lake with Windermere.

Normally I would have been thrilled by the prospect of spending time just walking around the magnificent fells, admiring the stunning scenery and absorbing the tranquil splendour of the place but on this occasion, there was a catch!

We had been invited by Mrs P's cousin, Reggie, to stay in his caravan!

Now I like Reggie, I like him a lot but sharing a caravan with him and Mrs Reggie, for five days???

Well you have to admit that in a caravan there isn't a lot of room for privacy or any chance of solitude, regardless of how big it is. That's not to say that Reggie does not have a big one, far from it because in the caravanning world Reggie claims to have a rather large one. He has never declared it to be the biggest in existence but quite rightly he is proud of its size and often compares its merits with other aficionados.

I am not an expert on the matter but when he has taken it out in the street to give it a good wash, quite a lot of people have shown an interest and inspected it thoroughly. He is usually delighted to show it off to neighbours or passersby and they have always been suitably impressed with its virtues. He does take great care of it and as I said, he cleans it on a regular basis, always ensuring that everything is in tip top condition and functioning perfectly before pulling it from its customary position.

Then once a year just before the season opens, a friend of his performs a meticulous examination of it, gives it a good greasing and then provides a full service.

Apparently he is very proficient and an expert in his profession but Reggie insists that he is also quite cheap, only charging the minimum rate and thereby guaranteeing fantastic value for money.

I know that Reggie has always been fully satisfied by his friend's performance and readily recommends him to other enthusiasts.

As well as being a large example, it is also very well equipped with everything that the modern devotee could ever want. Among the facilities it boasts are a fridge, freezer, LCD television, oven, microwave, blinds, fly screens, loose fit carpets, water tank, anti-theft tracker, TV directional aerial, stereo system, DVD player, external gas BBQ point, roof-light, shower, alloy wheels, extractor fan, cross actuation remote mover, cassette toilet, and a hitch head stabiliser.

Not that I know what the majority of those contraptions are, or what purpose they serve and obviously I have always been a little reluctant to ask, particularly in the case of the "hitch head stabiliser" and the "cassette toilet". I am only aware of their existence by having the really good fortune of knowing Reggie, who can prattle on about their qualities for hours, without ever pausing for breath.

You can imagine my reaction when having "downed" a couple of beers, he launches into his favourite subject. I always try to remain calm and let it pass over the top of my head but when "cross actuation remote mover" and "cassette toilet" are heard in the same sentence, I throw in the towel and lose the will to live.

So despite Reggie's caravan being a large luxury version, I was on the verge of declining his kind invitation.

My lack of enthusiasm however, was not solely based on the craving for my own space or even the limited amount of opportunity to escape from Reggie's eulogizes. It was also based on past experience and even though this knowledge was acquired some thirty years ago, I remember <u>most</u> of the incidents as if they were yesterday. Once when we were holidaying with Reggie in Cornwall, it never stopped raining for a week. All I could hear for days on end (apart from Reggie that is) was the rain hammering on the caravan roof. It made so much noise that sleep was impossible; inside was almost as damp as outside and I have never been so cold, even though it was the middle of July!

I am sure if Reggie hadn't chosen his pitch so meticulously, on top of a hill, we would just have floated off into the sea. The last sighting of us would probably have been as we rounded Land's End drifting towards America. Not that anybody could have seen us, not in all that rain.

Obviously, there are a multitude of other events all of which endorse the evidence and support my reticence about caravans and caravanning. These include the "sleep walking transvestite incident", "the swarm of angry hornets in the shower block episode", "the thong thing" and the "cock and sheep event." However even though all of these occurrences provide the necessary verification for my beliefs, it is better for everyone concerned if any further reference to them is completely prohibited.

So I had just told Reggie that we would not be accompanying him on his latest expedition when he disclosed his "bombshell."

Apparently the whole trip had been planned for my benefit and it had already been booked and paid for – by Reggie!

The chosen site was brand new, we were attending the official opening and it was the most luxurious every built. It was the Waldorf – Hilton – Astoria of the entire caravanning world. It had everything, heated indoor and outdoor swimming pools, Jacuzzis, solarium, saunas, gymnasium, games hall, ten-pin bowling, fishing lake, supermarket, 2 bars, pub, free cookery and craft lessons, hairdressers, beauty parlour, spa facilities, 2 restaurants each with a cordon bleu chef, shopping mall, golf course, and a theatre.

What's more and this was the clincher; Mark Knopfler was going to perform in the theatre and the entrance was free for all guests.

"Bloody hell," I said to Reggie as he told me the news, "Mark must be really in dire straits if he is reduced to playing in caravan parks."

Reggie explained however, that on the web site where he had made the booking, it said Mark was a friend of the owner and he was performing at the opening concert as a favour.

Most of my family know that despite me being a teenager in the era of Elvis, Cliff and The Beatles; I was more recently, a bigger fan of Mark Knopfler. From my first hearing of "Sultans of Swing" I was a committed admirer of his music and subsequently bought all of the Dire Straits albums. Then when Mark went solo, I continued to collect his recordings. In retrospect, I must be very boring because all my friends are aware that I thought his latest album "Get Lucky" was one of the best collections of songs ever produced.

I had been privileged to see Mark perform previously but only in huge stadiums where I was a least 50 yards away from the stage and this caravan trip would give me the opportunity of seeing him "up close".

Well Margaret Thatcher would have been proud of me and she could never have done a better job because a complete and total "U turn" occurred – I was going and wild horses would not prevent me.

I thanked Reggie profusely and over the next few days, I thought of little else. Reggie showed me photos of the park that he had downloaded and printed from the web site, it looked fabulous and I couldn't wait!

We made plans for the journey; Mrs P and I were to travel in our own car, following Reggie, Mrs Reggie and their caravan. The brand new resort was situated well away from any towns or villages but we decided against taking any food or drink because everything was available on site. All we needed to pack were clothes, swimming gear, fishing tackle, golf clubs, etc, and Reggie was going to use his Sat Nav to guide us straight to the complex.

The web site warned that no guests would be allowed admission before 4pm on the opening day but our eagerness took control and we decided to set off early to get a "prime site." The weather was good, the incessant rain of the previous weeks had ceased and the sun was shining brightly. The M6 was soon left well behind us, as we headed towards the heart of the lakes.

Then the roads we were directed to use by the Sat Nav became narrower and narrower. At one point, I flashed Reggie to stop and drew his attention to the fact that it was now impossible to turn his caravan around, should the "Sat Nav Man" be wrong.

He told me not to worry because his system was infallible, so onwards we travelled.

Then the "road" became nothing more than a track and a faint one at that but onwards we trekked. Eventually we stopped and Reggie jumped out, telling me that the Sat Nav said, "We had reached our destination".

There was nothing there – well there was a field, a huge one and it did have magnificent views but there was no complex.

The navigation system had made a mistake - it must have?? We tried switching it off and back on again but still it insisted we had reached our destination. The positional information was inputted several times but the result was always the same – we had arrived at our intended location.

We remembered passing a small farm house a few miles back and as Reggie couldn't turn his vehicle around while it was still hitched to the caravan, I was dispatched to ask if they knew where the "Lake District's Premier Vacation Resort" was situated.

Luckily, there was someone in the farmhouse but they didn't know of any nearby caravan park. So I explained that it was newly built and had only just been completed.

Patiently, they told me any new complex was not feasible because all of the land for twenty miles in any direction was designated green belt land, which meant any form of new build was completely prohibited.

Dejected, I drove back to Reggie who after opening the gate, was in the process of entering the field to turn around his caravan.

Then as I looked in my rear view mirror, I saw a caravan approaching and a little further behind yet another. Getting out of my car I climbed onto the gate and looked back along the track to see a line of caravans, all heading our way.

Had all the satellite navigations systems in the world failed or had everybody inputted the wrong information?

Reggie certainly couldn't take his caravan out of the field now because it was impossible for two caravans to pass on the narrow track. There was only one option; all of the approaching caravans would have to enter the field before anyone could leave.

With some reluctance Reggie's caravan was parked and then we watched as everyone followed our lead, by entering the field and parking. A small group of holidaymakers came and asked if we had any information regarding the "Resort". They were soon joined by more and before long there was a crowd of angry "holiday-makers" surrounding us and all wanting answers. Thankfully we were soon able to convince them that we were as much in the dark as they were and just because we arrived first, it didn't mean we possessed any more information.

Mobile phones were produced and it was discovered that a signal could be detected by Orange users but unfortunately not by any other network. A couple of calls later and our disgruntled band learned the facts - it was all a scam – there was no "Premier Resort." The photos posted on the web site had been taken at various other sites throughout the world. The golf course was actually in America and the outdoor swimming pool was in the Maldives. Mark Knopfler, who was also in America knew nothing about the complex or the proposed concert, the swindlers had just used his name. It was all a confidence trick and the perpetrators had disappeared along with the money paid by Reggie and our fellow travellers.

What could we do?

There was still the occasional caravan arriving, it was getting late and we were miles from anywhere. In addition, there couldn't be another site capable of taking all of the travellers now parked in the field. There was no other option; we had to spend the night in the field but the tricksters had done us one favour, they had chosen a beautiful spot for their deception.

So caravans were unhitched, awnings and tables were assembled, satellite aerials were rotated, BBQ's were set up and crockery was unpacked. Then it dawned on us, we had no food or drink because "everything was available at the resort" and it soon became apparent that we weren't the only ones in this predicament. There were quite a number of people who like us had been planning on experiencing the skills of one or both of the resident cordon bleu chefs. Word of the food shortages soon spread among our new community and then an amazing thing happened.

Those who had provisions began to get together to discuss exactly what they could make available and it didn't stop there. People were assigned to cook chips, others potatoes, several were allocated rice and several different groups were chosen to prepare salads, soups, steaks, chickens, pasta, burgers, eggs and bacon.

There was a real community spirit growing – everyone was in the same boat – having been swindled but everybody was determined to make the best of it. Bottles of beer, wine and spirits appeared and shared equally. Three men produced guitars and began to play. A female accordion player was joined by an old man playing a similarly old and battered squeeze box. A man and wife volunteered to sing, much to the delight of their young children and the remainder brought chairs and formed a circle. So with the impromptu band in the centre and the audience surrounding, our concert began. Soon we were clapping and singing, while others took turns to hand out the food and drink.

It was a magical night, the stars were shining brightly, it was warm and there wasn't a breath of wind.

We discovered that the guitarists were all friends who practised together quite regularly. We also learned they too were avid Knopfler fans who had been enticed to the venue by the promise of the unique intimate performance. So to make amends to other similar minded fans, they decided to play as many of their hero's songs as they possibly could.

The husband and wife team who offered to sing were semi-professional and had previously performed on their local folk circuit, before retiring to concentrate on their children. The old man with the battered squeeze box claimed to have played with Donavon and Jethro Tull in the early sixties.

Mrs P and I loved it and even Reggie who thinks that "Chirpy Cheep Cheep" is still in the charts tried to join in. We didn't want the night to end; there was something very special about it, almost miraculous.

Then to bring the concert to its ultimate conclusion our band played my favourite, "Piper to the End".

It was brilliant and a really appropriate finale to an incredible night. Slowly the audience dispersed, thanking the artists as they did so. We did the same but I was saving my special thanks for Reggie because I felt particularly privileged.

I remembered that initially, I hadn't really wanted to be part of this excursion, jealously protecting my privacy and preferring a little solitude. Now thanks to Reggie, not only had I seen a perfect example of the "Blitz Spirit" - I had also been part of it. I had witnessed stoicism and kindness at its finest, everyone standing shoulder to shoulder, sharing everything and attempting to make the best of a bad situation.

Everybody present had been deceived and duped out of their hard earned cash but then the best in humanity had bubbled to the surface and it had created a brotherly, compassionate and caring community.

We had all been looking forward to a first class concert and thanks to people's fortitude that's exactly what we got.

I slept very well that night, even though Reggie was snoring loudly only a few yards away.

The next day everyone began to pack, preparing to leave, there was no mad rush for the field gate, just an orderly queue. Two experienced caravan owners stood at the exit guiding and assisting fellow drivers to negotiate the tight corner. Other travellers who were waiting patiently to leave, waved happily at every caravan that departed.

Then it was our turn and with one last backward glance over the concert field we set off.

After we travelled about quarter of a mile, I said to Mrs P, "Well, we may not have not been lucky enough to have heard Mark Knopfler perform "Get lucky" but in the end, I think we really did get lucky".

I wasn't sure if she knew what I meant because there was no reply.

At home, the following day Mrs P and I were discussing Reggie's generous gesture of inviting us to the resort and the amount of money that he had lost because of the scam.

We were feeling very sorry for him and began to consider if there was anything we could offer him as compensation. "Take him for a weekend break, pay for his next holiday with Mrs Reggie or even pay for his caravan's next service," all of these ideas, along with many others were thoroughly debated. Unfortunately every notion we thought of, was for the future and we felt that Reggie needed something to bolster his feelings - now!

After a lot of discussion we decided to visit Reggie and give him all of the money that he had lost to the fraudsters.

Initially Reggie refused our offer but after a couple of beers he relented and agreed to accept half of the amount.

"A fair result for everybody", I thought.

Then with the effects of his fourth beer beginning to show, he announced that because he was once again feeling "flush" he would spend the money on a new luxury cassette toilet for his caravan. Apparently this latest version had a much larger capacity, a push button electric flush and even an LED display to indicate when it is full.

It would give him the ability to "go" wherever he decided to go and even on the go!

At that point I told Mrs P that it was time for us to "go", so we quickly left before Reggie could go into any more detail or even start lecturing me on the merits of the latest "cross actuation remote mover"!

Chapter Ten

September.

"Magic of the Dales"

"The promise of the Yorkshire Dales,
Is a lure that rarely fails,
And caring for a cat called Magic,
Could not possibly turn out tragic,
But things became a little weird,
When our "Magic" disappeared,
And the haze became a fog,
When I found that bloody dog."

Following another of her epic telephone conversations, Mrs P revealed that the caller was her Niece, "Olivia" who had asked us to stay at her house while she was away for the weekend.

Not surprisingly, I enquired, "if we are busy keeping an eye on your Niece's house who will watch our house while we are away?"

After being told not to be difficult, I was informed that we weren't looking after Olivia's house but her cat called "Magic," which wouldn't be any trouble because it only required feeding twice a day. Apparently, it was named Magic because it was entirely black from head to tail and Olivia loves Black Magic chocolates.

What's more, as Olivia now lives in the Yorkshire Dales, I was promised a "nice relaxing weekend with a few enjoyable rambles through the beautiful Yorkshire countryside."

We had visited Olivia previously, so finding her house was easy, even though it was located a few hundred yards from the road and could only be accessed by a dirt track.

Gaining entry wasn't a problem either because Olivia had thoughtfully left a key under a flowerpot and we soon discovered the cat in the kitchen, sleeping peacefully in its box.

At that point I remember thinking, "this should be OK - I can't foresee any problems here".

So while I carried the holdall, which contained our clothes from the car, Mrs P made us both a refreshing cup of tea.

It was while we were sat in kitchen, drinking our tea that things began to go wrong. First of all, I noticed that Magic was no longer in its box and a frantic search quickly revealed it was no longer in the house!

Obviously, Mrs P claimed the missing Magic was my fault because it could only have escaped while I was carrying in our holdall. This explanation certainly seemed the most plausible, so accepting the criticism and rebukes; I suggested continuing our search outside. The garden was thoroughly examined but there was no sign of Magic and because Mrs P was still complaining about my lack of cat caring qualities, I recommended we split up and hunt further afield.

She took the area between the front of the house and the road, while I examined the fields to the rear of the house. At least I couldn't hear her disapproving comments any longer but neither could I hear or see any sign of the cat. Then after crossing the second field, I came across a disused limestone quarry, which was quite deep and only protected by a barbed wire fence. Presumably the fence was to prevent cattle from plunging down but obviously it was completely useless in preventing cats.

I didn't believe for one moment that Magic could have fallen into it but decided to check anyway. After all, cats have nine lives and if they fall they always land on their feet, don't they?

So, even if Magic had fallen, it would still have another eight lives left – provided of course it hadn't fallen down the quarry previously.

Slowly, I scanned the bottom looking for any movement or any sign of the cat but there was nothing to be seen, other than the stone rubble. Dusk was falling and a hazy mist was starting to form on the quarry floor which made seeing anything quite difficult. So with the light fading and vision deteriorating, I was about to give up when I did see something but it couldn't be Magic because what I saw was definitely white!

It wasn't easy to distinguish in the haze and against the white of the stone but it didn't move and looked like a stuffed toy dog that someone had simply discarded. It appeared to have landed in a sitting position on the broken rock but as I walked around the edge of the quarry rim, I thought I saw its head turn, only slightly but enough to keep its eyes on me.

Had I imagined it?

It did look like a dog and I was sure its head had moved but how had it got there and why did it not bark or run around?

I was about to investigate further but just then I heard Mrs P calling, so I turned and retraced my steps, keeping an eye on the dog as I did so. Again I got the impression it turned to watch me but there was no other perceptible movement and it certainly made no sound.

During the walk back I met Mrs P who also confirmed her lack of success in finding the lost Magic. So with both of us troubled and feeling very concerned for the welfare of the cat, we returned to her niece's house. You can imagine our surprise and delight when we opened the kitchen door to find Magic back in its box and once again, fast asleep.

Elated but baffled we decided it was time for supper, which gave me the opportunity to relate my story about the toy dog to Mrs P. She was intrigued and said we should both investigate my claims the next day.

So the following morning, as soon as it was light enough and breakfast was finished, we set off for the quarry. The low mist was still present as I guided Mrs P to the spot where I had first seen the dog and sure enough, it was still there, in exactly the same position – sitting and looking upwards but at both of us this time.

It had to be a toy; no animal could possibly sit for so long without moving but unconvinced, Mrs P instructed me to repeat my stroll around the edge of the quarry while she stood motionless and watched. As I walked I got the same feeling that its head rotated ever so slightly towards me. Then Mrs P shouted, "It is a dog and it's alive!"

Before I had ran the few yards back to Mrs P, she had already decided that it must be injured, it was unable to get out of the quarry and more worryingly, I was going to climb down and save it!

Now for someone who has never climbed beyond the sixth rung on a ladder and begins to feel dizzy when going up stairs, the thought of climbing down the quarry face was to say the very least daunting but more honestly, bloody terrifying!

I tried to convince her that she was wrong, after all how could she tell that it was a real dog from that distance?

She wasn't Superwoman, she didn't have telescopic eyes or x-ray vision to see inside the dog but it was no use arguing, her mind was made up. So I examined the sides of the excavation to check if there was an easy route downwards, preferably one where I would still be alive when I reached the bottom.

Then I saw my opportunity - at some time previously, part of the quarry wall had collapsed, creating a stone ramp almost to the quarry floor and although the angle was steep, it could possibly be negotiated, provided I was very careful and extremely lucky.

Very slowly I descended and even though the stone was loose in places, the ramp seemed quite stable - well stable enough for my weight at least!

With the minutes ticking by and Mrs P shouting encouraging remarks from the safety zone beyond the barbed wire fence my confidence grew as I moved steadily downwards. In some places I sat down on the rubble and eased myself along, just like I had done all those years ago when sliding down the slag heaps but the difference was, the technique was now being employed to prevent me sliding.

Then with one final jump and a huge sigh of relief, I reached the quarry floor. So waving cheerfully up to Mrs P, I walked the short distance towards the dog. It hadn't moved, it was still in the same position but its head wasn't tilted upwards in the direction of the quarry rim anymore because its eyes were still fixed on me and now we were both on the same piece of rock. It was a small, sturdy looking dog with a broad face and covered from head to tail with long white flowing hair. Its dense white coat seemed to emphasise the blackness of its eyes, nose and lips.

As I moved closer it began snarling, displaying its sharp white teeth and then it attempted to bite me - thankfully without success but only because it seemed unable to move from its sitting position.

Having seen the numerous animal training programmes on television, I believed talking would have a comforting effect but the sound of my voice only appeared to increase its anger. I went to stroke it but every time my hand went anywhere near, a new attack was launched.

The dog had made its mind up - I was the enemy and under no circumstances was it going to allow itself be lifted and carried to safety.

Yet we were just as determined to help and as we didn't know how long it had been there, without water or how long it would take to get someone to help, we needed a plan.

I shouted up to Mrs P to go back to the house and bring our holdall, (the one we had used to transport our clothes) and some gloves, preferably thick ones!

She willingly disappeared and soon returned with the items, throwing them down extremely carefully, so as not to hit the dog but without any thought for me.

She had done brilliantly and found a pair of very coarse leather, gardening gauntlets.

Pulling them on, I pushed my coat sleeves down as far as possible, so that no bare flesh was visible and unzipped the holdall.

Then quickly lifting the dog (which immediately sank its teeth into my left glove), I put it in the holdall and closed the zip just enough to leave its head outside, still snarling and still with my hand in its mouth.

After a few seconds, I managed to extricate my hand and inspect the damage, the teeth marks were visible but luckily my skin wasn't broken. Then I noticed my four legged enemy wore a very small collar and from it dangled a tiny disc but even though I still had the gloves I wasn't going to risk examining it, at least not yet!

So placing the holdall's strap over my shoulder and with the dog's head facing away from my body, I began the difficult climb back to the top of the quarry. I stopped a couple of times to rest but the going up seemed a lot less hazardous than the descent, even though I was now also carrying the dog.

Mrs P helped me for the final few yards back to the barbed wire fence but her concern was entirely for the dog and not the tooth marks still visible in my hand, or the numerous scrapes that I had collected during my mountaineering exploits.

Miraculously the dog offered no resistance as Mrs P examined it. Then turning the disc she read, "Hektor" followed by a telephone number.

Back at the house, the first thing I noticed on entering the kitchen was that Magic was missing – again. This time however, I definitely couldn't be held responsible because it was still asleep when I left for the quarry and as I immediately pointed out, the only person who had been in the house since, was Mrs P!

The cat however was forgotten, as our priority now was the welfare of the dog. I removed "Hektor" from our holdall but as he seemed to have much better relationship with Mrs P, I let her offer him some food and drink before she dialled the telephone number found on his collar.

Almost immediately the call was answered by a woman with a foreign accent, so Mrs P explained that we had found her dog but it was very distressed and could be badly injured because it was unable to walk.

It soon became apparent that the woman's command of English was fairly basic but she did understand that we had found Hektor. Making her understand our location or comprehend any directions however, was a completely different matter, so Mrs P eventually gave up and offered to take the dog to her.

It was decided we would meet her at Ilkley railway station, a place which the woman knew well and not far from her home but a place which was over twelve miles from where we had found her dog.

It transpired the woman was a very beautiful Polish girl named Anka who had only been in England for the previous four months. As both Mrs P's and my Polish is not that good, Anka had thoughtfully brought along a friend who was also Polish but could speak fluent English and she helped to translate.

We learned that Hektor was a pedigree Shih Tzu who had been missing for five days and Anka had paid over £500 for him. She had been searching night and day for him and had even printed and distributed "Missing Dog" posters.

There was no explanation of how the dog could have ended up in the bottom of the quarry, or why it was such a distance from its home but Anka and her friend thanked us both profusely.

Feeling very pleased with ourselves, Mrs P and I returned to the house where the elusive Magic was once again back in its box, fast asleep.

That night before we went to sleep, Mrs P and I had only two topics of conversation; one, how did the bloody cat get in and out of the house and two, how did the unfortunate dog end up in the bottom of the quarry?

The next morning during breakfast the phone rang, it was Anka who had noted the number from our call the previous day.

Thanking us once more she asked, "Would we meet her again at the railway station".

Mrs P agreed, so back to Ilkley we went and as we parked, Anka and her friend came running towards us. As a reward for finding Hektor, she had bought us a present in the form of cream cakes - but they weren't just ordinary cream cakes - they were special cream cakes.

As her friend explained they were a Polish delicacy called Kremówka Papieska or "Papal Cream Cakes". Apparently they were a favourite of Pope John Paul II who ate them at every opportunity and because of his endorsement they were now the preferred dessert of the whole country.

How could we refuse?

So giving Anka our home address and telephone number, we asked to be kept informed of Hektor's progress and returned to Olivia's house once more but this time armed with our cream cakes.

Obviously the cat was missing but it didn't seem to matter much any more. After all, we knew that somehow Magic could come and go as it pleased but it would always return for mealtimes or sleep. We ate the cream cakes with our supper and of course they were exceedingly good cakes - they couldn't be bad or naughty cakes with such a heavenly testimonial - could they?

I thought that would have been the end of the story, apart from possibly receiving updates on the progress of Hektor's recovery but I was soon to be proved very wrong.

Now, I have no proof of any link between the Papal Cream Cakes and the condition of our bodies the following morning, which incidentally was also the day we were supposed to be returning home but.................

Both Mrs P and I awoke with terrific griping pains in our stomachs, nausea and a very high temperature. Then as the morning progressed, the vomiting began and so did the diarrhoea. We were both too ill to drive home so there was no option, we had to stay put.

The next few hours were a bit of a blur but sometime during the late afternoon, Olivia returned home. After assessing our symptoms, she drove to the nearest chemist for medicines and then insisted, "We stay with her for few days or at least until the medicine had chance to work".

Two days later both Mrs P and I were beginning to feel a bit better and as Mrs P joked there was no need for us to go on a diet or visit the gym anymore to lose any weight. So that evening, we decided to return home to the comfort of our own beds.

During the drive we tuned the car radio into a news bulletin from a local Yorkshire station, which said that there had been a number of food poisoning cases in the area and that a delicatessen in Ilkley was suspected of being the source.

Now as I said previously, I have no proof of any link but...........

We had almost reached home when Mrs P remembered that in our haste to leave we had completely forgotten to ask Olivia how Magic was able to come and go so easily from the house when both of the doors were shut.

I told Mrs P not to worry, we would find out next time because the "nice relaxing weekend with a few enjoyable rambles through the beautiful Yorkshire countryside" that I had been promised, never materialised and had probably disappeared with Magic.

Then after thinking about my comment, I said that Magic was a very suitable name for that cat but "Houdini" was probably a better one.

Two weeks later, Anka phoned to say that Hektor was almost fully recovered and was well enough to take part in his favourite pastime of attacking any passing animal or human. Apparently, she had named him after a Greek prince who was considered to be the greatest fighter in the Trojan War and the name Hektor means "holding fast".

I also considered him to be very well named because of the fight he put up against me and the way he "held fast" to my gloved hand when he sank his teeth into it.

Over the next few months we became quite friendly with Anka and with her English improving rapidly, we decided to see for ourselves just how well Hektor was doing.

During our visit, Anka invited us to stay for lunch and served us "Zupa Jarzynowa," which she explained is a type of chicken and vegetable soup, followed by "Pierogi" which are dumplings filled with mushrooms and meat.

Both Mrs P and I thoroughly enjoyed the meal but when it came to dessert we both made our excuses and left.

During the drive home, I said to Mrs P that we weren't religious enough to cope with another rich helping of the Popes Cream Cakes and for once - she agreed.

Mr Pensioner

Chapter Eleven

October.

"Over the Borderline"

"I was starting to feel the pressure,
Cos Mrs P claimed she's from Cheshire,
I thought she might be going deranged,
Ever since the boundaries changed,
But now I know, it was all a ploy,
Conceived just so, she could annoy,
I always knew that she weren't posh,
She simply never had the dosh,
So if you speak with her accent,
You're from Lancs, so be content,
But there's one, with a strange disorder,
Who should be inside, with a warder,
Same as those who changed our border,
Because they too, were Out of Order!"

I suppose it is a symptom of getting old but Mrs P and I had been reminiscing about "The Old Days" and in particular, we had been discussing our childhood and the neighbourhood where we played as kids.

We were both born in Lancashire and less than twelve miles apart but thanks to a Local Government Act in 1974, the village where Mrs P was born is now in Cheshire and my birthplace is now part of Greater Manchester.

As a result Mrs P believes that she now belongs to the posh Cheshire Set and I am just referred to as the "Manc". Due to this reorganisation, proud industrial towns like Wigan, Leigh,

Bolton, Bury, Oldham and Rochdale were swallowed up to become part of the Greater Manchester "Metropolis" while Warrington, Widnes and others became part of Cheshire.

It wasn't just our area that was removed from Lancashire however, as more towns like Southport, St Helens, Bootle and Wallasey all became part of the new Merseyside Metropolitan County and further north some of the Lancashire Lake District was taken by the new Cumbria.

It had always been my belief that Lancashire not only lost some of its towns, it also lost part of its history and heritage during this reorganisation.

Wigan is a prime example; it claims to be Lancashire's oldest town, being of Celtic and Roman origin. In 1246 it was awarded a Charter by King Henry the third and became a Royal Borough. During the Civil War it stayed loyal to the King and was the scene of various battles. In the eighteenth century it was a spa town where people came "to take the waters".

Later farm workers moved in, hoping to prosper with the new industrial age and mills multiplied on the banks of the River Douglas. Then the surrounding fields were covered with mines, slag heaps, waste and railway tracks as Wigan became the archetypal industrial town where the Kings Cotton and Coal ruled.

At the height of the coal mining industry, Wigan was said to have over 1,000 pit shafts within a five mile radius of the town centre. Nowadays most of the mills have disappeared, the last coalmine closed in 1992 and the land once poisoned by heavy industry has been cleared, landscaped and redeveloped.

Wigan was made famous in different ways by the words of George Orwell and George Formby but the town is not alone in having a notable history. All of the towns relocated to other "administrative areas" have equally significant histories. George Formby was proud to have been born in Wigan, "the deepest, darkest part of Lancashire" and I wonder what he would say now, to find it is part of Greater Manchester.

Not that the government of 1974 or any government since has really accepted that the County of Lancashire has been reduced. They stated at the time, "The new county boundaries are administrative areas and will not alter the traditional boundaries of counties, nor is it intended that the loyalties of people living in them will change despite the different names adopted by the new administrative counties." This rhetoric has been repeated many times over the years but the old boundaries are being forgotten and youngsters now refer to themselves as living in Merseyside or Greater Manchester, rather than being Lancastrians.

I suppose the media is to blame for a large part of the confusion as it refers to these "administrative counties" rather than the geographical counties. Listening to BBC Radio Lancashire on a Saturday afternoon you will receive commentary on Preston North End's game but to listen to Bolton's you must retune to BBC Radio Manchester. Watching "News from the North West" on TV, the presenters always refers to incidents happening in Chorley, Lancashire or Horwich, Greater Manchester. Even the BBC is guilty of condensing Lancashire in size and alienating its residents. Our heritage is fast disappearing, soon the new generation of Pie Eaters from Wigan, Keaw Yeds from West-houghton and Sparrows from Lowton will never know that they are really Lancastrians.

I wonder what would happen if we had to repeat the War of the Roses, after all Yorkshire still consists of North, South, East and West Yorkshire and collectively they are a significantly larger than what is left of Lancashire.

While I bemoaned the fact that the younger generation now considered me a "Manc", Mrs P relished the idea of being elevated to the upper echelons of Cheshire. I think the image of all those luxurious houses, designer shops, elegant restaurants and expensive cars were beginning to have an effect and she seemed delighted with the notion of being associated (however remotely) with its affluence. Her village might have been miraculously transplanted into the "administrative county of Cheshire" but it was nowhere near the "Multi-Millionaire Triangle" of Alderley Edge, Prestbury and Wilmslow. I told her, "Cheshire might be considered one of the most sought after places to live in the UK and attract people wanting to live the dream with a "fabulous Cheshire lifestyle" but she could never be considered a true native and anyway Posh and Becks no longer lived there".

Was it the thought of all of those millionaire businessmen, footballers like Wayne Rooney and Rio Ferdinand or the soap opera actors that appealed to her so much that she was ready to denounce her Lancastrian heritage?

She was too old to be a footballer's Wag, there didn't seem to be that many actors of her age in Coronation Street, there certainly wasn't any in Hollyoaks and Families finished years ago – not that I could ever remember her watching it.

So what was the attraction of Cheshire and why was she so thrilled to now be considered a native, albeit a naturalised one? After a great deal of interrogation, numerous probing questions and yes, several large glasses of white wine, she finally admitted that it was all a ploy. All these years she had pretended to value the concept of her being born in Cheshire but it was just a hoax. It was a deception she had perfected just to irritate me because she knew of my loyalty to Lancashire and the Red Rose.

In reality she was delighted to be just like Gracie Fields, a "Lassie from Lancashire" - well probably not a lassie considering her age but with her accent, she was definitely a Lancastrian!

All of which left me thinking, "who was ever brave enough to inform Gracie that Rochdale was now part of Greater Manchester," because the changes happened in 1974 and she only died in 1979?

The following day when Mrs P had sobered up enough to cook breakfast, we continued our discussion. She remembered being about three or four years old and learning that baby Jesus lived in Bethlehem. Knowing that Bethlehem was a long way from her home, she believed it was "across the fields," just the other side of the East Lancashire Road. Obviously to a young child, walking the half mile to the A580 would seem a long distance, so it was only natural she should believe it was the location of Bethlehem. In my estimation that would place Bethlehem somewhere near to the centre of Croft, which historically was in Lancashire but now is part of Cheshire.

Did this mean Cheshire had a claim on the birthplace of Jesus as well?

I responded by telling her that as kids we had a rope swing that was fastened to a tree and swung high over a fast running brook. Normally we took turns in swinging to see who could get the highest but one particular day three of us were on it, attempting for a joint world record. Unfortunately the rope broke and we fell about ten to twelve feet, landing in the brook below. The water was only about twelve inches deep, so we were very lucky that no one was badly injured but we were completely drenched.

Only a brief discussion was needed to decide that we couldn't possibly go home so wet because the consequences were too great. Our parents may let us get away with going home dirty but dirty and soaked to the skin - none of us were willing to take that chance!

There was no option, we had to dry our sodden clothes before we dared to venture home and because teatime was only an hour away, we had to dry them quickly. One of the older boys who hadn't been on the trapeze at "break-time" produced some matches and after a few minutes we had a fire going. We stripped off most of our soggy attire and then found twigs and branches to make a clotheshorse, on which to hang them.

Things seemed to be going well and I thought steam was beginning to rise from our garments but more wood was piled onto the fire to speed up the drying process. After all, we couldn't afford for any girls to come wandering by and see us in this state, only wearing our still wet vests and underpants.

Then we heard the dreaded shout, "Girls coming" and all of us, including the ones still fully clothed made a dash for the bushes. Totally hidden from view, we listened for the recognisable chatter of girls but there was nothing.

We waited in silence, ears straining for the faintest sound but only the birds singing and a slight breeze rustling the leaves could be heard. Minutes passed before we cautiously emerged, our senses still on high alert for any sign of the opposite sex but it was just a false alarm.

Walking back, we were laughing and joking about the event but when we arrived at our fire, the laughter stopped and our amusement was replaced by despair because our clothes had been set alight and they were badly burned!

Not totally destroyed but certainly enough for us to realise that we were in deep, deep trouble!

During our absence, some of the branches in the fire must have toppled towards our temporary clotheshorse and caused the disaster.

One leg of my trousers was burnt almost to the knee, while my shirt had several scorch holes and a cuff was missing. I was much luckier than one of the others though because he suffered serious damage to his trousers, shirt and socks but even worse, the toe of his left boot was completely gone.

I had tea standing up that night and I think my friends were also unable to sit down but worse than the punishment or the chastisement was the fact I had to return to wearing short trousers again.

My mother cut off the good leg on my burnt trousers to the same length as the scorched one and produced me a pair of short pants. During the following months everyone would remember our bonfire by the sight of my shorts, until thankfully I tore them to shreds when sliding down one of the nearby slag heaps.

So the discussion progressed, each of us taking turns to narrate a tale from our childhood despite the fact that over the years we had repeated the very same stories many times. I told Mrs P again about us damming the brook, performing "danks" and falling out of trees, while she recounted her adventures of potato picking, falling through the conservatory roof and having live frogs put down her blouse by the boys – a prank from which she has never fully recovered.

Then we began to realise that even though both of us were very familiar with each other's stories, we had never shown one another the actual locations of our escapades. So we decided to use our concessionary travel passes and visit the sites of our childhood exploits.

As my birthplace was nearest to our present home, I would have the honour of being the first guide, then later we would travel to Mrs P's village for her tour.

So next day, just after nine thirty (the official starting time for pensioners' travel) we joined our fellow aged travellers on the almost full Arriva bus.

Alighting near the park, I showed Mrs P the actual tree from which our trapeze hung, the tree that Billy Morris fell from when he broke both arms, the pond on which we unsuccessfully attempted to float our homemade raft, the pond where "Gulliver" the biggest fish in the world lived and the spot where we all paid a penny to watch Stan Jones first kiss Nellie Boardman.

Not only was it the first kiss for Stan, it was also the first time any of our group kissed a girl because until then we had done our best to avoid all contact with "soppy girls". After all they liked dressing up or playing shop but they were totally useless at making fires or jumping brooks. However, it wasn't long before most of our gang followed Stan's lead and began allowing girls to accompany us on our adventures.

That morning, I managed to show Mrs P most of the locations where my stories took place and as we walked more memories came flooding back.

As soon as I saw the old bridge, I remembered us all using it to cross the brook but rarely did we walk across, no that was far too easy. We would hold on to the underside of the bridge and dangling like apes, we would attempt to traverse. Obviously the crossings weren't always successfully negotiated but the drop to the brook was just a couple of feet and only socks and shoes would normally get wet.

The remains of a dilapidated wooden fence jolted my memory of how we tried to walk like tightrope walkers along the top of it. Our circus act kept us occupied for days as we all sought to be the champion by travelling the greatest distance before falling.

Unfortunately, that particular competition was very quickly abandoned after Jimmy Jackson slipped and landed very heavily with a leg either side of the fence. The high pitched scream Jimmy emitted could be heard for miles as he sat motionless on top of the fence, with his chin pressed into his chest.

It took four of us to roll him off and onto the ground where he stayed on his knees, with his forehead in the grass and hands plunged deep into his nether regions for what seemed ages. I don't think any of us ever tried tightrope walking again after that, well certainly not on the top of a very solid wooden fence.

The only site that I was unable to show Mrs P was the spot where we would dam the brook because for some reason over the years at that particular point, it had changed course. The steep banks that I remembered had gone; presumably washed away, leaving the modern stream now several times wider. To be honest, I believe that we must have contributed to the bank erosion, which produced the alluvial plain that was now evident and if we were capable of that with a small stream, just think what we might have accomplished if we had lived near a real river that we could dam, like the Nile or Mississippi.

My tour was at an end and it was now Mrs P's turn to show me the "sites" but because of recent changes to village bus routes we now had to go by train. Our concessionary passes would still allow us to travel free for most of the journey but because Mrs P's hometown was now in Cheshire we had to pay for the part of the excursion that was "over the borderline".

We emerged from the station nearest to Mrs P's village and walked the mile and a half to her childhood play area. First I was shown the site of the famous frog incident, followed by the place where her gang caught field mice. Apparently each gang member took one home to be their latest pet but luckily, Alan Jones's father found out and released all of them back into the wild.

Next we visited the location of the old orchard where Mrs P would "scrump" apples but it was gone and in its place was a mock-Georgian mansion, surrounded by an eight foot high wall complete with electric gates and CCTV cameras.

A similar fate had befallen the tree, which had formed the basis of their den. Mrs P thought it used to be situated in what was now the kitchen of a five bed roomed detached house that had recently been constructed.

One of the two farms where she roamed had gone and houses now occupied the land but the old barn was still there, although that too had been converted into a home. The other farm had survived and was thriving even though part of it was now trading as a garden centre. However the main business was still farming and the field in which Mrs P had laboured by picking potatoes was still cultivated.

Our last location was the pond where a young Mrs P and all of the people living in her neighbourhood would go swimming during the long, hot summer days.

Apparently the pond had a gently sloping sandy shelf that was totally free of pot holes, weeds, or rubbish and it was extremely safe for bathers. She recollected that on very warm days, as many as thirty people would be splashing about in its waters or simply sunbathing on its banks.

It was completely surrounded by trees, which sheltered it from any breeze and hid it from the view of any casual passersby. This concealment and setting gave a sense of exclusivity, making everyone feel privileged just to be relaxing in its tranquillity. She always described it as an idyllic place and now after all these years, I was going to see it at last.

It was situated about three quarters of a mile away but across the fields we could clearly see the wood concealing the pond, which Mrs P had always described so affectionately.

Unfortunately the track used by the bathers all those years ago had gone but as I told Mrs P, this was perfectly understandable. With the numerous heated swimming pools and health spas that had been built in the last fifty odd years, no one would either risk, or need to go swimming in a pond anymore. Mrs P however, remained adamant that in her day the now invisible track was a public footpath and not just used by bathers!

So in the absence of any official signs or stiles with which to cross from field to field, we skirted around the perimeter of each meadow. Then we either climbed a convenient gate or crawled through a break in the hedgerow to enter the next field. Gradually, we zigzagged towards our destination and before long we had reached the outskirts of the wood but still there were no noticeable paths. Neither were there any obvious signs of people ever using the area but with Mrs P leading and pushing her way through the bushes, we continued our search for the pond.

Then suddenly we were through the trees, into a clearing and there in the centre was the pond - or to be more exact what was left of it. The sandy banks which Mrs P had described were gone and so to presumably, was the gently sloping bottom. The clear, cooling water remembered with such fondness had been replaced with a black, muddy sludge and it looked dreadful. There had been some attempt to drain it and rubbish had been tipped, presumably to reduce it in size. Around its edges, branches and brushwood had also been dumped, possibly to deter any fishermen, although I doubted very much, if any fish could have survived in those conditions.

We both stood in silence, taking in the ghastly scene with Mrs P transfixed, attempting to comprehend the transformation and the reasons for it.

Then suddenly we heard a shrieking yell and looking up from the pond we saw a figure stood at the opposite side of the clearing, gesticulating angrily at us.

He strode towards us still shouting, so slowly we walked to greet him. He was dressed in a dark green hunting jacket, brown corduroy trousers, long brown boots, checked shirt and a green tweed tie with a matching flat cap but more worryingly, he held a shotgun over his left arm.

When he reached us, he was still bellowing and he accused us of trespassing. Calmly, (well as calmly as I could with what I presumed was an irate farmer brandishing a shotgun three feet away) I apologised for being on his land and explained we were just out "site seeing" for the day. I assured him we had not left any gates open or done any damage but he became even more agitated and began shouting something about poachers.

Initially I didn't realise that we were the poachers to whom he was referring, so very helpfully I glanced around to try and catch sight of any illegal hunters. There were none to be seen and it began to dawn on me that we were in trouble because the crazy character opposite really did believe we were poaching.

Not that Mrs P or myself were dressed for poaching or that we had anywhere to hide our kill even if we had been hunting. Well to be honest, Mrs P did have her handbag but with everything else she already carried in it, there wasn't much space left, so we would have had difficulty even squeezing in a small mouse.

It was very obvious he was a little weird - not exactly eccentric - more what you would describe as "peculiar" but at least he had finally stopped yelling. So in an effort to foster better relations, I took off my coat and showed the oddball that I wasn't hiding anything under it and Mrs P opened her handbag for him to look inside.

Gradually he began to believe in our innocence and told us that he had been having trouble with illegal hunters.

I asked how the pond had got into such a terrible condition. He replied by telling us that he had done it to prevent people from picnicking on its banks.

As I was thinking what sort of "nutter" would destroy such a beautiful spot, he revealed that he had bought all of the surrounding land several years ago and wanted to keep it totally private. The fields were no longer farmed but were used solely by him and his friends for "country pursuits" which he claimed meant hunting, shooting, clay pigeon shooting, and 4X4 racing.

Beginning to feel a little more relaxed but still keeping a watchful eye on his shotgun, I said that I thought this a very good idea on which to base a business and all he needed to do was open it up to the paying public.

Immediately he returned to his dark, ill-tempered mood and shrieked, "That's the whole point - I don't want ordinary people like you two, tramping all over my estate".

I could see there was no sense in discussing the matter further, so to change the subject as quickly as possible I enquired where he lived before he bought the land.

Very proudly he announced that he was both born and bred near Wilmslow in the "Heart of Real Cheshire".

Without thinking, I asked if he recognised and knew Mrs P because she was also born in Cheshire and was therefore a compatriot of his.

I could see the rage building inside of him, his nose twitched and the index finger on his right hand began to tremble uncontrollably. He was on the "borderline" of exploding and I thought the slightest wrong word would push him over, so I promised we would leave his estate immediately and never return.

On our way back from the pond we didn't take the trouble of zigzagging our way around the field perimeters, we simply took the shortest route possible.

Periodically I would glance back over my shoulder to see him still watching us with his gun over his left arm. He had followed us through the wood but stopped on its outskirts, at a point where he could observe us all the way back to the road.

I believed our "remembrance day" of "site seeing" had been entirely marred by an upper class snob who probably hadn't worked a day in his life and treated everyone but his friends as totally inferior. He was jealously guarding his land and attempting to prevent others from enjoying what had obviously been a very beautiful spot but in doing so, he had turned it into an environmental disaster.

When we reached safety, I said to Mrs P, "You Cheshire Set might live your lives just over the borderline but he was over the borderline of sanity, by a long way".

We decided to call in the nearest pub for some refreshment and also to regain our composure. It was late afternoon and the pub was empty apart from the landlord who was sitting at the end of the bar, reading a newspaper.

Seeing us enter, he jumped to his feet and began serving while Mrs P chose a comfortable seat in which to relax. As he pumped my pint of "Timothy Taylor's" he said, "I haven't seen you two in here before". I quickly explained that I was from over the border but Mrs P was a true native of the area. Then I went on to tell him a little about our recent encounter with the "shotgun carrying estate owner".

"I know exactly who you mean," the landlord said, "he comes in here sometimes, pretending to be Lord of the Manor, you should keep away from him – he's a nutcase".

Given the confirmation that my opinion of the "Lord of the Manor" was correct and that he was indeed a little crazy, I decided to relate a little more detail regarding our latest acquaintance to the landlord.

He listened to my story without interrupting but as I continued, I could see he was becoming increasing agitated.

When I finished my tale there was a brief silence as the landlord took a deep breath before revealing that the gunman had no friends, nobody ever visited him and certainly no one ever accompanied him on hunting or shooting trips. He had never worked but bought the land about fifteen years ago, just after his father had sold the family scrap metal business and given him most of the money.

Then I was astounded to hear that the gunman wasn't from Cheshire at all but was actually "born and brought up" on the outskirts of Wigan, where his father's scrap yard was located!

So he wasn't from "over the border" after all, he was from Lancashire just like me and of course Mrs P!!

But obviously that was only until they moved Wigan into Greater Manchester!

Which I said definitely made him a "Manc" and obviously "MAD for it"!

125

Chapter Twelve

November

"Justice 4 us 2"

"One man's word, is just one man's word,
Justice needs that both be heard,
It was a waste of time, I felt,
But Spanish justice should be dealt,
Then they tried to tell us both,
There is no need to take the oath,
Cos he's made a change of pleas,
And now begs mercy - if you please,
We never knew, just what he got,
But it cost us two - quite a lot."

It was November and having landed safely at Malaga airport (thanks to Easyjet), we were back in Spain. It was much cooler than on our previous visit but we weren't there to enjoy the weather because we were there simply to attend the trial of the Moroccan thief.

Now for the benefit of those who may have to experience any similar situations, Malaga's City of Justice is on the outskirts of the city and quite a distance from the airport. The best way to get there is to catch the train from the airport to Malaga Central terminal (Alameda) and from Alameda catch the L20 bus towards the University. Be warned though because the bus could be packed, not only with students but with all sorts of walking wounded, as it also passes the hospital along the way. I suppose "walking wounded" is a bit of an exaggeration as during our journeys several people who couldn't walk without the aid of friends and crutches were manually hoisted on and off the bus. It appeared the nurses working in the fracture department that day were having a competition to see who could plaster the largest area of any patient.

The cost of a return train and bus journey from the airport to the City of Justice is quite reasonable, at a total of 9 Euros per person. It can also be accomplished relatively quickly as trains leave the airport every 20 minutes, buses are every 8 minutes and the courts are only a few yards walk from the bus stop. Once through the airport style security examination and into the justice building, it is a relatively simple matter to find the correct court, just check the "destination boards".

As usual not knowing how long the journey would take, Mrs Pensioner and I arrived early, in this case over an hour early but we benefitted by each having one of the very scarce chairs which were positioned outside the court.

Slowly the area filled and some familiar faces arrived, four were the uniformed policemen who helped us and another was my "saviour". We waited with anticipation for the appearance of "Mrs Christmas" but as the minutes ticked by without her arrival, I was delegated by Mrs Pensioner to ask the policemen of her whereabouts.

Would you believe it! She was on her honeymoon; apparently she had fallen head over heels in love with the strange, bespectacled man who materialised when the thief was apprehended.

It seems she was now a changed ~~man, person,~~ woman gone were the sulky, sullen looks, they had been replaced by jolly, cheerful smiles. In fact there hadn't been one complaint or grumble from her in the last six weeks and she was now considered to be the life and soul of the station.

It occurred to me that I was the catalyst for this miraculous event; if it wasn't for my instigations they would never have met, there would never have been a wedding and all of the policemen in Fuengirola would still be living in fear – not to mention some of the criminal fraternity.

Should I set up a dating agency, the Spanish equivalent of that Match Dot Com thingy, which I keep seeing advertised on the telly? I made a mental note to contact Joe down at the club as soon as I returned to England; he is always saying how good he is with them computer things. After thanking everyone again and asking for our good wishes to be passed on to Mrs Christmas, I returned to my precious seat to wait.

Mrs P was just telling me that she thought that the thief would fail to show up when he sauntered in, accompanied by his legal representative. Looking in our direction they had a "brief" conversation, whispering to one another with hands over their mouths. Perhaps they thought I could now lip read Spanish from 30 yards!

Then the lawyer began his work, first he shook hands with all of the police connected with our case and had a few minutes chatting amiably with them, possibly exchanging jokes. Then he repeated this interaction with the court usher and other officials before returning to his client. The two of them had another brief discussion, then the lawyer returned to his new "best friend" the court usher and together they walked into the court. They were gone about five minutes before the lawyer returned and held another meeting with his client.

This scene of the lawyer going backwards and forwards between the court and the robber was repeated numerous times in the next thirty minutes and you could safely say that Mrs P was becoming more than a little disconcerted. So taking matters in hand, she confronted the court usher and asked for an explanation. As soon as the necessary translator arrived, we learned that the thief was "plea bargaining". A short time later we found out he was now pleading guilty and as a result our evidence wouldn't now be required.

We were then invited into the court by the "judge"; it turned out there were three of them, sat in a "U" formation. They thanked us for attending the court, told us the thief now recognised his wrongs and he would be sentenced later. We in the meantime were free to go, so with a, "enjoy the rest of your day" we were dismissed.

We never discovered what happened to the thief or the sentence he received; perhaps it was better that way, Mrs P would only have ended up worrying about him.

I thought however, that with us spending all that time and money in returning to Spain, at least they could have made arrangements to inform us.

I suggested going back in to the court room and asking the judges to "let us know" but Mrs P dissuaded me by promising me a few drinks in the nearest bar.

On the bus back to Malaga centre I noticed for the first time that Mrs P's locket was not visible. Had she lost it, forgotten it or simply decided not to wear it?

Whatever the reason it was a first because as I said previously, the locket was the constant in our lives having been worn every single day since 1973.

"Where's your locket?" I gasped, obviously thinking the worst. With a smile, she pulled down the neck of her blouse to reveal the familiar gold chain. Then with her right hand she reached to the back of her neck and withdrew the locket.

She was still wearing it but hidden and down her back!

I told her she was being silly, the chances of it being stolen here were the same as it being stolen anywhere else, even in Manchester!

Was she going to wear it hidden for the rest of her life?

Back in Malaga centre and with several hours to wait before our flight we decided to kill some time by going to a cafe for tapas.

I took the opportunity to try and convince Mrs P that it was impractical for her to continue concealing the locket and she should either wear it normally or not at all. After some debate and a very large glass of red wine she reluctantly agreed and displayed the locket as usual. Walking to the train station however, I noticed that she was looking suspiciously at every passerby, almost treating them as potential thieves. Again I told her not to be silly and relax because she was perfectly safe - well as safe as she could be anywhere!

It was rush hour by the time we reached the station and the platform was crammed with people, all wanting to get home. As we waited in the crowd for the train to take us back to the airport Mrs P became even more anxious and began to finger her locket very nervously.

Eventually the train arrived but it was packed and with every seat taken, Mrs P and I were forced to stand in the carriage along with a large number of other people.

I became aware of an Arab-looking man (probably Moroccan given the proximity of that country to this part of Spain) staring intently at Mrs P. She had also noticed him and with a fearful look on her face was once again touching her locket apprehensively. Suddenly the man stood up and quickly strode the few yards towards Mrs P. Her left hand had closed firmly around the locket and her right hand was clenched at shoulder height. Poised she was ready to deliver her knockout blow. I too was prepared for the tussle and was about to intervene but something in the Arab's manner made me pause. Then directly in front of Mrs P, the man stopped and said something in Arabic (I think) before turning and pointing towards his now vacant seat.

He was offering Mrs P his seat!!

"Thank goodness for that," I whispered with relief.

Immediately the atmosphere changed and Mrs P's anxiety and tension completely disappeared.

She gratefully accepted his seat and thanking him profusely (in English but with a Lancashire accent) she gave him a huge smile. I will never know if the Arab understood what Mrs P said but he returned her smile and she continued to smile all the way home.

I shall always be grateful to the anonymous Arab because I sincerely believe it is thanks to him that Mrs P not only continues to wear the locket but she also wears it in its normal position – at the front and on display!

A couple of weeks after returning home from the trial In Malaga, I began to reflect on the theft once again and it was then that I recognised the irony of the incidents.

After all it was a Moroccan who initially caused our difficulties by stealing the locket and it was almost certainly another Moroccan who recovered the situation by offering his seat to Mrs P.

Chapter Thirteen

December.

"Sub-versive Do it Yourself Incarceration"

"Our Daughter's house was once a pub,
Famed for its beer and delicious grub,
But now the decor was that tired,
A major upgrade was required,
Without complaint we did the work,
There was no task that we did shirk,
Good relations we had tried to forge,
With Justin and my "best mate" George,
And there wasn't that much to do,
When the dogs asked, "can we help too?"
But now were all locked in the cellar,
Don't know how - we're going to tell her."

Our daughter and her husband had recently bought a 200 year old house, which began life as a pub. It had been transformed into a home during the 1980's but now it was in need of another major upgrade.

They were living in it whilst conducting renovations but as both were fully employed, the amount of time they could devote to their project was limited. As Mrs Pensioner and I now had plenty of spare time, it seemed logical that we should help out. So a couple of times a week we would travel the short distance to their home and carry out our allotted tasks. Sometimes we were simply asked to take delivery of materials, or oversee specialist contractors but occasionally we were trusted to carry out some of the actual remedial work. Consequently, during the previous months Mrs P and I had scraped off countless rolls of ancient paper, removed hundreds of tiles and chiselled off several tons of plaster from the inner walls.

In addition, we had removed fireplaces, chimney breasts, yards of skirting board and lifted numerous floorboards. Then we had sanded and varnished floors before fitting new lights and curtain rails.

Our work hadn't just been restricted to the inside of the property either, as during the summer months, when the weather permitted we had also been requested to work in the garden.

One particularly arduous job was the complete removal of a privet hedge. I know this doesn't sound exceptionally challenging but this hedge was over twelve feet tall by six feet wide and must have been growing when "Adam was a lad". First we cut the branches down to a height of about two feet then excavated the roots, before lifting and finally removing the offending bushes.

What a job, it took us five days of hard labour but eventually the hedge was consigned to the tip.

A similar process was undertaken for several trees with one removal being particularly memorable. Over two days, we had reduced the troublesome tree to the customary two feet height. Then to undermine the roots, we had dug a hole over six feet diameter by about three feet deep when a sudden torrential downpour began.

Despite the rain, we decided to try and finish the job but water started to fill the hole faster than we could remove it. Our daughter's two dogs then thought they would help us and jumped into what was fast becoming a small pond. The dogs must have got the idea we were looking for bones because the scene became something like a Disney comedy. With the dogs digging away with their front paws, spraying sludge everywhere while we chopped and pulled at roots in the pouring rain.

Finally, when the two dogs, Mrs P and I were totally drenched and covered from head to foot in mud, the job was complete.

Please don't think we disliked the jobs we were asked to do – far from it – because we loved doing them and wouldn't have missed or changed a single task. In fact, we looked forward to them with great anticipation and as soon as one activity was finished, we would make suggestions for the next, in the hope of us being commissioned. As a result there had been lots of occasions when we went home totally exhausted physically but feeling terrific mentally.

Over time we got to know the contractors who came to work on the house and we learned of their personal problems or aspirations. We knew who preferred coffee to tea and how many sugars they needed. We also became acquainted with the workers at the local tip because we visited it so often when disposing of the waste.

We began to recognise some of the drivers who delivered the materials and accepted their peculiarities, like George and Justin who both worked for B&Q.

The first occasion I met George, Mrs P had gone to buy curtain material, leaving me alone and "in charge".

We had ordered twenty of the largest sheets of plasterboard and George had been designated to deliver them. Due to "Health and Safety" regulations however, George was "only allowed" to drop them thirty yards from our daughter's door. Obviously I was a little disgruntled and told him so but he was adamant that he had to adhere to the letter of the law and H&S ruled.

Muttering under my breath, I reminded George about the clown who was banned by the H&S from wearing his brightly coloured, size 18's clown shoes because he might trip and fall.

I then explained that the reason the clown wore the big shoes was for him to appear humorous and also to make people laugh when he tripped. Now thanks to Health and Safety, he was protected from tripping but he was also out of work because the circus could not afford to pay a clown who couldn't do his job.

Regrettably the significance of my tale and any similarity or parallel was completely lost on George. So conceding defeat, I thanked him for delivering the boards so close to their intended destination and as I had been left in charge, I made the executive decision of moving the plasterboard indoors, just in case of rain.

Now, the weight of one large sheet of plasterboard is not that great but because of their size they are a little awkward to transport by a single person and just to make matters worse, it was an exceptionally windy day.

So now – and partly thanks to George - my task had become extremely challenging because not only had I to carry each board nearly forty yards but I also had to do it in the face of a very tricky wind.

Cautiously, I lifted the first board and successfully manoeuvred my hands to balance it. Then very carefully I walked the thirty yards to the house entrance but as I turned to go through the door the wind struck. Acting like a sail, the sheet took the full force and propelled me several yards past the entrance. Luckily I managed to prevent the board from hitting anything and it remained intact, however forcing my way back to the doorway, took quite an effort.

During the next nineteen trips I became fairly adept at assessing the strength of each gust. Then using this evaluation I calculated the point at which I needed to turn into the wind so that I could terminate each of my short flights at the doorway. Utterly exhausted, I had just carried the last sheet into the safety of the house when Mrs P returned with the curtain material.

A few weeks later we needed another twelve sheets of the same plasterboard and to be honest, I wasn't looking forward to it being delivered, even though the weather was good.

Fortunately this driver - Justin - was different.

I could tell immediately as he stepped from his cab that Justin was completely different.

From his immaculately pressed bib and brace overall with the creases down the legs to his paisley lilac shirt with the cuffs turned back, Justin was not the same as George.

From his perfectly coiffed and streaked blonde hair, to his gleaming black boots, Justin was poles apart from George – like chalk and cheese.

"Where do you want it?" was his first question.

Somewhat apprehensively I replied, "Where can you drop them?"

"For you, I will drop them wherever you want," he responded.

Beginning to feel a little better about the distance I would have to carry the sheets but with other concerns now creeping into my mind, I said, "Inside would be better for me".

"I don't mind it being inside," he replied.

Remembering George, the previous driver, I asked, "but what about Health and Safety".

"Don't you worry about that, I always wear the right protection," came his answer.

"In the hallway would be good," I naively suggested

"As long as there is enough room for us, in the hallway it is," he agreed.

Amazingly, he then transported all of the sheets into the house by himself.

He refused all of my offers of help, saying it was part of his job description and I would only get plasterboard dust on my "lovely trousers."

He was going to stay and have a "nice cup of tea" with me but he suddenly remembered he had an urgent delivery to make, when Mrs P appeared.

So after advising me to thoroughly moisturise my hands before handling the plasterboard because it played havoc with his skin, he left.

"What a nice man," I remember thinking after he had left, "What a difference between him and George, if only all deliverymen were as accommodating as Justin."

This particular day, however both our daughter and her husband were working away. She was attending a meeting in Birmingham, only returning home late and he was staying overnight on a two day training course in Sheffield. In their absence, Mrs P and I had been given the very simple job of positioning an extra radiator in the kitchen.

It wasn't a big job and we weren't even required to link the radiator into the existing heating system. Our brief was simply to position and fasten the new radiator onto the wall, "run" the copper piping through the floor into the cellar and terminate it close to another radiator. With little plumbing involved and no need to drain the system, it was an easy job and we fully expected to have accomplished it in a couple of hours.

"With luck", I thought, "we might even finish the job, take our daughter's dogs, Kyba and Jay for a walk and still be home in time for lunch".

Things were going well and with the help of the dogs who insisted on jumping on us, licking us and pawing whatever we touched, the new radiator was in place. Even the holes in the floor that would accommodate the copper tubing had been drilled.

All we needed to do now was to go into the cellar and secure the pipes. Working together, Mrs P and I had almost finished the job when the two dogs came bounding down the cellar steps. Obviously, they were missing us because it was now almost ten minutes since they had last seen us in the kitchen. In their haste to greet us and discover just how they could be of further assistance, they inadvertently released the catch, which retained the cellar door.

With a crash it fell, triggering the locking system as it did so.

We were now locked in!

There was no other way out and it was no use shouting because there was no one to hear us!

Mrs P blamed me, I blamed Mrs P and we both blamed the dogs but in effect we were victims of our own success because it was us who had modified the door to make it so secure!

At the time, we had good reason for our "safety conscious handiwork" but now I was regretting our decision. Previously when the house was still a pub, the beer barrels were lowered into the cellar from what was now the house driveway. Although this entrance had been permanently sealed a few years ago, we considered it as still being vulnerable to a forced entry. So to prevent access to the upper part of the house by anyone who had broken into the basement, we had strengthened the cellar door and it was now rock-solid.

Consequently, I knew it was pointless trying to force our way out and our only option was to wait for our daughter to return home.

We were imprisoned in our own private Alcatraz, so how would we spend the time and how would we cope?

My thoughts went to the Chilean miners who had been trapped underground, we were experiencing just a little of what they had gone through.

I half-remembered a training course which I attended many years ago when I was still working. It was on the subject of "brain training for positive thinking" – could I use anything of what I had learned to put a positive perspective on our predicament and produce a satisfactory outcome?

The course claimed that our brains were designed to keep us alive and we are driven by instincts which click into action when we sense danger. These instincts are called the 5 F's - flight, fight, food, fornicate and freeze and apparently all of them are essential for the survival of the human race. I couldn't really remember in what circumstances they were meant to be applied but I knew that fornicating or even the slightest mention of it wasn't going to help our situation, not in the mood that Mrs P was in. It might keep us from freezing to death, which was another of the essential "F's" but it would better to save that particular "F" for just a bit longer, at least until relations improved a bit.

My stomach began to rumble, another of the "F's" was kicking in, even though we had only been imprisoned fifty minutes and lunchtime would still have been another hour away.

Trying the positive thinking approach, I told myself it wasn't that bad, things could have been a lot worse. We had light, we had plenty of room, it wasn't that cold and we had the dogs to keep us company. In addition, we also had water because it seeped into a tank that was situated in the corner, before being automatically pumped into the drainage system.

I might have had my optimistic head on but I still told Mrs P, "I would have to be really desperate before I resort to drinking that."

Shakespeare had once said something about us creating a prison by our own thoughts, so in a way he agreed with my training course - we had to stay positive. In reality there was no danger and therefore no need for the "5 F's" survival instincts.

The cellar roof was certainly not going to collapse, well not for the next fifty years at least and the risk from escaping gas or explosions was minimal. We certainly wouldn't starve to death, although we may get a little bit peckish in the next few hours and of course there was always the ground water in the corner.

It might be true that nobody knew exactly where we were but it was only a matter of time. So all we had to do was wait patiently for our rescue.

Again my thoughts went to the Chilean miners, their conditions and all of the comforts they had been denied during their ordeal. Trying to put myself in their shoes, I began to list what I would do, if I was rescued after being trapped for the same amount of time in equivalent conditions.

Seeing all of my family and friends definitely came top, followed by having the longest, hottest shower ever, sleeping in the most comfortable bed with the cleanest, freshest sheets imaginable, and feeling the cool, fresh air on my face in the widest open space that I could find.

It occurred to me that if my list contained the things I would do after being deprived of my freedom and everything I treasured, then these must be the same things I considered were the most important in life.

So family, friends, washing, sleeping and breathing fresh air were my most valued experiences but coincidently they also cost very little in monetary terms. As my list contained no expensive desires, it made me appreciate not only just what was really important in life but also how much the miners must have suffered and endured. It was not the loss of a 40" plasma TV or being deprived from driving the latest red Ferrari that caused the most suffering but the loss of simple things in life like daylight, fresh air, clean clothes, peaceful sleep and family.

The hours passed slowly, after all there are only so many things you see can in a cellar and only so many times you can play "I Spy" without it becoming too repetitious.

We let the dogs drink some of the water but avoided it ourselves and of course we finished fastening the heating pipes.

At one point we both believed we heard footsteps above us but after further deliberation we conceded that it was our imagination. It was either that or my positive vibes were beginning to produce the "satisfactory outcome" my training course had predicted but in what ghostly form, I wasn't sure.

In the end my optimistic thoughts never materialised anything to grant us our freedom, so there was no early release but eventually our daughter returned from Birmingham. She realised we were still in the house by the fact that our car was still parked outside but decided to search upstairs first, despite our frantic shouting.

We were liberated at last and the elation was immense.

We had only been in our prison for a few hours, so if we felt that good, how did Nelson Mandela feel when he was released from prison?

Nevertheless, we had survived and "done our time", even with or without the help of the "5 F's"

After a couple of cups of steaming hot coffee, from Brazil - I think - not Chile and some bananas, which Mrs P (the nurse) said would be good for our digestion and energy levels, we decided to drive home for the precious hot shower, change of clothes, supper and of course that peaceful sleep.

I don't think we were incarcerated in our underground prison long enough to begin missing friends or family and in any case Mrs P had been with me all along.

Our decision to return home was even more certain when our daughter informed us she could make us some Chile Con Carne and it would only take a few minutes......

During the drive, I remembered the training course once again and thought, "Should I try to persuade Mrs P into practising one of the 5F's before our peaceful sleep?"

After some very careful deliberation, I totally dismissed the idea and settled instead for telling Mrs P to think positive and look on the bright side.

After all we had already realised our ambition and achieved our goal of spending "<u>time</u>" and doing things together......

145

Chapter Fourteen

Conclusion

"There isn't a stadium,
Or any such medium,
From which to look at life,
But when troubles are rife,
Take advice from a wife,
Cos answers "you" strive,
Are for "us" to derive,
And choices "we" make,
Are all for "our" sake."

"You cannot teach a man anything, you can only help him discover it within himself" – Galileo.

So that's how our first year in Pensionland ended, with us accomplishing our goal, albeit in a way that we never intended when we first discussed our aspirations.

Twelve months previously, the thought of "gaol" being defined as "prison" or "doing time" had never entered our heads. We had spoken the words; "goal", "doing", "time", and "together" all in the same sentence but during December our words had been rearranged and we had "done time together in a type of gaol".

Nevertheless, we had successfully fulfilled our ambition and obviously in more ways than one but in achieving it we seemed to have suffered from a tremendous amount of bad luck.

Our year had been strewn with incidents and accidents but misfortune didn't appear to be limited simply to us. It also seemed to extend to the people who came into contact with us, such as the mole catcher and the woman at the therapy centre.

During the first six months Mrs P and I had been soaked to the skin, covered in mud, trapped by a car and suspected of drug trafficking.

In the second half of the year, things got really bad when we were robbed, subjected to fraud, bitten, poisoned, intimidated by a gunman, then soaked and covered in mud again before finally being imprisoned.

Yet these were just a few of the ill fated events in which we were involved because as I made clear at the beginning, I was only going to reveal the details of one occurrence from each month.

In reality there were so many incidents that we considered this year as our "Annus Horribilis".

So was the fact that Mrs P and I were now spending more time together the cause of these strange happenings?

Were Mrs P and I similar to the constituent parts of a bomb, which when kept separate pose no threat but mixed together become extremely dangerous?

On the other hand we had been together for over forty years and in that time we hadn't experienced too many difficulties. We had encountered problems of course; all families do but no more than our fair share. So were all of our recent exploits simply coincidences or was realising our ambition always destined to be riddled with disaster?

Thinking back to March and our encounter with the mole catcher, would he have been catapulted from his quad if we hadn't intervened?

Striving to answer the question, I reasoned he would definitely have set off on his ill-fated journey a few minutes earlier if we hadn't delayed him with our queries but surely he would have taken the same route because we had neither affected his starting point nor his destination.

This meant his accident would still have occurred and our meeting with him could only then be described as lucky. After all, if we hadn't been in the vicinity his mishap would have gone unnoticed and he could have lain in considerable pain with a broken leg for a very long time.

In reality it was us who raised the alarm, Mrs P who attended to him and we both helped to carry him to the ambulance.

Previously it seemed our strategy of "spending time together" was totally jinxed but now I had proved that our involvement with the mole catcher was incredibly fortunate - for him at least!

So could I use the same philosophy on the other occurrences?

Well certainly our encounter with Hektor the dog was very lucky, both for him and his owner Anka.

Then I realised that we were also very lucky because by finding Hector we had also found a new friend in Anka.

This reasoning could also be applied to the mole catcher who since his recovery had visited our home and even offered to remove the uninvited mole that had taken up residence beneath our front lawn – "completely free of charge."

Now I know there are "mates rates" but I think only true friends offer their services completely gratis!

So it was certainly a lucky day for everybody concerned when we chanced upon the mole catcher!

Slowly as I analysed each of the other events, I began to realise how fortunate we had been and just how lucky we really were.

Obviously, I had always believed that we were very fortunate to have participated in the Caravan Concert, where in the face of adversity everyone had "pulled together" to produce something truly memorable – a genuine caring community.

A caring community is a group of people from different backgrounds sharing a philosophy, which enhances services and resources, resulting in better outcomes for everyone - and that is exactly what occurred on the night of the concert.

Originally I was seeking solitude rather than the company of others but I was wrong because the feelings of camaraderie, friendship and "togetherness," I experienced will never be forgotten. That evening I understood what Cicero meant when he said, "We were born to unite with our fellow men and to join in community with the human race" but I wasn't the only person to undergo a change of attitude at that concert.

Initially everyone was angry because of the fraud but when that concert ended those same people travelled home feeling so much better about life and with valuable lessons learned.

This led me to consider what other lessons had I learned from the year's events.

Initially it was the tangible things that came to mind, like the Gara Rufa fish, I certainly knew a lot more about those than I did twelve months ago.

I had learned a little about mobile phones and their contracts, I also knew the Taj Mahal is considered to be romantic, moles are attracted to sheep and that mole hills are dangerous. I had also been taught how to carry a stretcher correctly and I had learned the principles of using a car jack.

Then I remembered our imprisonment in the cellar and while contemplating and empathising with the plight of the Chilean miners, I had recognised the experiences which I considered to be important in life. I valued family, friends, washing, sleeping and breathing fresh air.

I also accepted that other people's values may differ and mine may change over time but I still felt fortunate for having had the experience of the cellar and grateful for the precious insight.

Suddenly I realised that I had experienced other principles and virtues, which were just as valuable - if not more so.

The stout lady we met at the therapy centre had a fish phobia. Due to the nature of the phobia, it didn't impact much on her everyday life and she could have easily avoided the potentially frightening situation by simply cancelling her treatment. Instead she demonstrated a great strength of character by deciding to face her fear. By doing so she also created an opportunity to cope with her phobia and possibly control it.

On the day, things didn't go well and her scheme didn't quite work out the way she hoped. Adopting a more gradual approach, rather than just "diving in" may have been more beneficial but by simply being present she had displayed courage of the highest order.

After all courage is doing something that you are really scared of doing and as Mark Twain once said, "Courage is the mastery of fear not the absence of fear". Her action of attending the therapy centre and actually "dipping her toes in the water" was equivalent to a First World War soldier "going over the top".

So I had witnessed and recognised "courage", which is the first and most important of all human virtues because without it, no other virtue can be practiced.

I knew that another of the virtues was justice and I had also been involved with that recently, especially when we visited Malaga's City of Justice.

Everyone believes they know what justice is, even kids, after all how often is a child heard complaining, "That's not fair"?

People often grumble that an action is unfair or unjust and they also automatically believe that the injustice will be seen by everyone else but what appears to be obvious to one person is not always apparent to others. Everyone agrees that justice is fundamental but they rarely agree on how it translates into practice and even two parents hardly ever agree on the correct punishment for their aberrant child.

"Justice is being fair and equitable in proper moderation between self-interest and the rights and needs of others," but who has set the benchmark for fairness and who has defined the standard by which these rights and needs can be measured?

It is presumed that they have been decided and set by the laws of each country and therefore justice is administered according to these same laws.

In some countries, stealing is punished by amputating the thief's hand, which to me is not "proper moderation" but obviously to the populations of these particular countries it must be, otherwise these countries and their residents are not believing in, or administering justice.

So both justice for the "wronged" and a suitable punishment for the "wrong doer" although linked, mean completely different things to different people.

Neither are justice and punishment simply administered according to each country's laws because the perception of their correct benchmark is also influenced by an individual's religion, culture, politics and philosophy on life.

Most justice systems operate with the structure that if a law has been broken, then a punishment must be administered. This seems a very costly exercise and one where only a few people can ever be fully satisfied with the outcome. For as I said previously, even parents can't agree on what is just or fair for their children, so one of them is usually upset with the result of the judgement.

In these times of economic hardship, justice needs to be balanced and cost effective but who measures the costs and who evaluates the benefits?

If a cost / benefit analysis was to be conducted on our case in Spain, the costs would be astronomical and I can't envisage how anybody could have benefitted whatsoever. Simply listing some of the cost activities performed solely on our behalf, I believe validates this notion.

The capture of the thief included the cost of six police officers, our hospital examinations and the generation of all the necessary paperwork. Next day our statements were taken, which involved two police officers, a translator and more paperwork.

There was the initial trial in Fuengirola where the thief pleaded not guilty and that required four police officers, two adjudicators, a translator and yet more paperwork.

There was the main trial which involved five police officers, three judges, the thief's lawyer, our translator, all of the court officials and obviously another mountain of paperwork. Then there were our costs for flights, accommodation, etc.

So who benefited?

Well certainly not Mrs P or myself because we had to pay all of our own costs, including the cost of a replacement chain for the locket. The community of Andalucía didn't benefit because they paid for everything else and I find it difficult to see how the thief benefited.

So, as there was no apparent benefit, should I simply have let the thief steal the locket?

After all its value is only around £300 and we spent more than that in attending the trials.

Therefore recovering the locket actually cost us more than it would have cost us to lose it.

So was our encounter with justice worth it?

Was all of the time and money spent by everyone involved, really merited?

Were the costs of administering justice really "justified"?

Would the money have been better spent on doing something more beneficial for the community?

If the thief hadn't been caught, there wouldn't have been a breakdown in society, life would have continued just the same and the money spent on administering justice could have been used much more constructively.

I suppose the question really is, "What price does the community put on justice?"

For the people to answer they need to know and understand which qualities they value and in what order of importance they place these qualities because only then can a justice system operate alongside and in harmony with these values.

Of course what my simple cost / benefit analysis doesn't take into account and cannot, are the intangibles, such as the memories the locket held and what it symbolised.

Now, who can put a price on those?

Certainly not me!

Then I remembered our encounter with the "Cheshire gunman". Was he guilty of practising Social or even Environmental Injustice by what he had said to us and what he had done to the pond?

After all Social Justice could be defined as, "complete and genuine equality for all" and Environmental Justice could be defined as, "giving all people – regardless of their race, colour, nation, origin or income – the ability to enjoy and protect the environment."

I will leave the verdict up to you but remember the land was his and presumably he could do what he liked with it.

We all live our lives according to some type of justice system - in our family life, in our work, in our neighbourhood, and even in our relationship or interaction with others but I don't believe that everyone will ever totally agree on how to administer or manage justice.

Nevertheless, I now considered myself fortunate to have been involved with and learned a little about the virtue of justice during "Our Year", although I am still not convinced the cost of justice is always totally justified.

In February I visited our local library in an effort to find out about "romance" and the art of being "romantic". I am still not exactly sure what I learned but I realise now that the most romantic present you can ever give is a huge red cuddly, teddy bear which has a big pink heart pinned on its chest. Onto this enduring symbol of love the words, "To my darling Valentine," must be written in scrolled gold hand writing. Obviously the teddy bear has to be holding a single red rose in one hand and a candle in the other but remember the gift can only be presented just as a blood red sun is setting in a golden, glowing sky with a string quartet playing "Unchained Melody" softly in the background while Barry White grunts the lyrics.

How anybody can ever have a blood red sun setting in a golden glowing sky during the middle of February in Britain is still beyond me?

Surely somebody will realise this soon and move Valentine's Day to the middle of July when there is a much better chance of experiencing such a sun setting paradise.

Yet I must have learned something during my investigations because by the middle of July I was playing cupid when I introduced "Mrs Christmas" of the Malaga Police to the "strange bespectacled man". Either I possess a natural skill with a bow and arrow or I was incredibly lucky with my shot because soon after my instigation they married and disappeared into the blood red Spanish sunset.

So once again our good fortune becomes remarkably apparent, after all how many people can claim to have prompted the ultimate match, which created the greatest love story and resulted in the perfect marriage. Now you have to be exceptionally lucky these days to achieve wedded bliss and not many people can claim that.

As that very famous guitarist but not so well known theologian Jimi Hendrix once said, "When the power of love overcomes the love of power, the world will know peace."

As I now have a proven track record in the "Lurve Business" and know so much about romance and the art of being romantic, I think my idea about setting up my own Match Dot Com agency isn't such a bad one.

Maybe I should I call my dating agency Mr P's Passion Parlour for Pairing Pleasure Pursuing People or Mr P's SIX P's Dot Com.

If however my plans for the dating agency never materialise, at least I can demonstrate that I learned a little about the virtue of love and just how lucky I was with love during our first year in Pensionland.

They say, "Patience is a virtue", strictly speaking I am not sure that it is but our patience was sorely tested during December when we were incarcerated for nearly nine hours in the cellar. The definition of patience is "the ability to wait for a long time without becoming angry or upset" and in reality that is exactly what we demonstrated. Initially both Mrs P and I were upset, blaming each other, as well as the dogs for our situation.

It was when we accepted that any early escape was impossible and when we recognised freedom would eventually come that our confinement didn't seem to matter anymore.

Originally, we had set ourselves a target of finishing the radiator task within a couple of hours but in reality it didn't matter how long it took, so what was the point of becoming upset or losing patience about it?

While considering the incident in December, I recognised similarities and parallels occurring throughout our year of "spending time together." We had made plans that didn't always work out but slowly we had begun to expect the unexpected and as a result we were more prepared to face the ups and downs of life.

We had become focused on the most important things in life and we were trying to be happy and grateful.

Then I realised that my favourite and most used phrase of the time was, "I am just happy to be here".

If you think about your own happiest memories, they will probably include occasions when your patience was rewarded. Would those memories be held in such high esteem, if you weren't proud of the result and the patience you exercised in their accomplishment?

Most good things in life take time and an abundance of patience is required to achieve them. If patience is not present then goals cannot be achieved, ambitions cannot be realised and expectations cannot be completed.

Everything cannot go according to plan, so don't expect it to, be prepared for the unexpected, be patient with yourself as well as others and remember losing patience can never make anything better.

In May I trusted the TV weather girl when she promised a beautiful day and obviously for me she got it wrong but for most places in the country it was a beautiful day.

So was I wrong to trust her?

Well she had made her prediction based on all of the available evidence at her disposal and there was nothing for her to gain by getting it wrong. So yes, I should have trusted her and my faith was well placed because as I said, for most places she did get it right.

It has crossed my mind however, that perhaps we are a little too lenient with weather forecasters and instead of just allowing them to predict rain, shouldn't we insist on them saying where, when and how much?

By doing so, the "rain" part of the forecast would typically be, "two inches of rain is expected to fall tomorrow in Manchester city centre, it will start at eight o'clock in the morning and finish by three in the afternoon; outside of the city centre there will be no rain until further notice". We could then measure what they predicted against actual conditions and produce a league table showing their accuracy. The public would then have a much better chance of knowing how much trust to put into any particular forecaster's prophecy. For example if Laura Tobin is top of the league with a 65% forecasting accuracy and Fred Talbot is bottom with 40%, we can calculate just how much faith and trust to place into each forecast.

Trust is defined as, "having a firm belief in the reliability, truth or ability of someone or something".

OK, my thoughts regarding the weather forecaster's league table may be a little whimsical and flippant but it's because "the truth" is often difficult to distinguish that we need boundaries and measures to build trust in relationships.

It is because we are all afraid of being subject to fraud, cheated, lied to, or simply let down that trust is not easily developed and it is for the same reasons that a framework with boundaries is required.

Thinking back to April and our encounter with the "Mobile Supplier", was there anything in his attitude, demeanour, conduct, image or appearance for him to convey trust?

He was late, forgetful, vague, shifty, scruffy and difficult to contact. All those attributes made one suspect that he was a very dubious character but he had something which made Mrs P trust him and in return he trusted her.

After all he gave her the 100% legitimate, working phone and took the money without ever counting or even glancing at it.

It is essential that prejudice and discrimination are never allowed to cloud judgement because everyone deserves a fair chance, both to trust and be trusted. It is only when people keep breaking promises that trust should be withdrawn but remember even then, that mistakes do happen and everyone deserves a second chance.

Mr and Mrs Cross who owned the village shop knew all about trust. They trusted their customers to return to their shop and pay for goods the following day or even after their customers' next pay day. They were also very wise because they had built a business on a platform of trust and with it, created a loyal customer base.

Being wise is defined as, "being prudent – having a deep under-standing and realisation of people, things, events or situations."

I wasn't exactly sure what was meant by being prudent but I had always associated the word with Gordon Brown and his budget speeches. Due to this connection and the way Gordon Brown referred to "Prudence," I thought being prudent simply meant "being cautious" and "not taking risks", so I decided to "research" the word.

I learned that Prudence is another of the virtues and is defined as, "having wisdom and showing good judgement in practical affairs".

More simply, it is exhibiting common sense and good judgement as well as utilising experience in any decision. I believe that is exactly what the Cross's demonstrated with their business model and they must have got something right because some of their strategy now forms the basis on which modern supermarkets operate.

Although considering some of the supermarkets actions I am still not sure they have fully grasped the ideology behind the Cross's approach to business. The Cross's developed trust, formed relationships and created customer loyalty. It is much better to have the luxury of repeat business, rather than making one sale and then desperately seeking another new customer for the next sale.

New customers are hard to obtain, keeping your existing customers is easier and forming relations with them is a step towards creating loyalty.

A business needs to create a competitive advantage and it achieves an advantage when it does a better job than its competitors at satisfying the product and service requirements of its market. It is when the customers' needs are satisfied that they develop a positive attitude towards the business, its products and its services.

I find it difficult to accept that any long term business can survive with just the minimum of customer interaction and by simply saying, "We are the cheapest".

Of course new ideas replace old ideas; that's how the world changes and you may argue that I am old and because of this, I cannot accept change.

Well, I recognise that change is inevitable, it is the natural way of things, like my hair changing colour to grey but should we accept all changes?

The Cheshire gunman had changed Mrs P's idyllic pond and its beautiful surroundings into an appalling environmental catastrophe and that particular change could never be considered good or acceptable. If all changes aren't for the better, then all changes shouldn't be embraced or accepted. There seems however to be a common confusion between "change" and "progress".

Progress is "to advance, improve and develop". To make progress, changes are needed but not all change is progress.

Therefore it is progress which we should be striving for and not change. Any changes which do not promote progress should not be accepted and any changes that prevent development or permanent progress should be fiercely opposed.

It is essential to develop new ideas but we also need to build on the experience and wisdom of those who have trod the same path previously and aim for progress not change.

After evaluating the numerous shopping excursions that we have completed during the last twelve months, I still have reservations about the way some companies conduct their business but I am extremely pleased with my promotion to "Mrs P's Assistant Loader of Checkout Belt" and I am looking forward to <u>progressing</u> even further.

I also realise that Mrs P was incredibly fortunate not to receive any serious injury when she was hit and trapped in the supermarket car park by the "Stiff Necked Driver," and how lucky it was that our car was not damaged.

Previously we had referred to our First year in Pensionland as our "Annus Horribilis" but with the examination of our escapades complete, I finally appreciated our good fortune and our extraordinary good luck. I had altered my perception of "Our First Year" and in doing so I had a more optimistic attitude to life; and my phrase of the moment, "I am just happy to be here," took on even more relevance.

My analysis of our year had helped us learn from life's challenges, turned bad situations into good and negatives into positives. What at first viewing was a jinxed year, strewn with trials, tribulations and troubles was in fact an amazing year full of opportunities, good luck and good fortune but more than that, it was also a year of discovery and learning.

We had seen and learned about "Courage" thanks to the Stout Lady in the therapy centre, "Prudence" in relation to the supermarkets and "Justice" from our exploits in Fuengirola and Malaga.

Courage, Prudence and Justice are three of the four Cardinal Virtues on which civilisation, morality and civilised thinking are based, so we had been very lucky indeed to have had the opportunity of learning about them.

In addition we had also experienced and learned about "Trust" from the Mobile Supplier, "Love" and "Romance" in our encounters with the Kettle and Mrs Christmas, "Change and "Progress" from our Shopping Excursions and "Patience" by being locked in the cellar.

Some of these qualities are also occasionally referred to as virtues, which they may or may not be but I am absolutely certain that they all possess virtuous merits. Further examination reveals other virtues and qualities to be found within "Our Year" but I will leave their discovery to you – trusting you have the patience and prudence to identify them.

Thanks to our change of outlook, we now considered "Our Year" a total success and we were extremely pleased with the results. We were still "getting on well with one another" despite the fact that we were now in each other's company for almost every hour of every day and we had also proved that we "worked well together" as a team, under pressure, in stressful situations and in a crisis.

We are currently looking forward to another successful year of setting goals and once again one of our aims will be "spending time together" because even in retirement, goals and ambitions are still required.

We no longer need to meet difficult business targets but re-tirement can still be very demanding and if you really want to achieve everything you hope to, then planning needs to be done and goals need to be set.

Very simply, "Goal Setting" is a case of identifying what you want to achieve, prioritising your aims, listing the steps needed for their achievement - within a timescale then evaluating progress and resetting aims if necessary before assessing and enjoying your success.

It is similar to having a map of exactly where you wish to be at any set time but the route and timescales for arriving at your intended destination are decided by yourself.

It is my belief that the "Ultimate Goal" for any human being is to be happy and therefore every aim or ambition we have should lead us towards this goal. However it is also my belief that while we all should attempt to achieve happiness in our own lives, it is better still if we bring happiness to others.

Remember the Caravan Concert when everyone was "pulling together" that action created happiness for all because everybody contributed.

We are all influenced by the community in which we are born, brought up or live and in return we shape and form the community around us.

Therefore, just as in business, it is essential that good relationships are forged with everyone and by using the virtues and qualities as experienced and recognised above, we all make changes and progress, for the benefit of ourselves, our families and our community. However, be mindful of what I learned in the cellar that some of the most important things in life are not always the most expensive.

Having read my story I hope you will now understand the reasons why we have adopted a more cautious approach to "doing things together" and precisely why we now take extra care.

I also hope that by reading my tale you have gained some knowledge, even if it is only to avoid us, for although we remain vigilant, we currently see every incident as an opportunity to experience or learn something new.

So if you see us out walking, digging up trees, fishing, shopping, caravanning, dog walking, poaching, running or simply just chatting in the street, approach with caution and **be careful - very, very careful**.

Ah, but I hear you say, "You haven't mentioned "The Chase" in your analysis, so why did you tell us about that?"

Well, what do you think was the point of the telling you?

Am I advocating that everybody should resist their muggers?

Do I believe everyone should attempt to stop armed bank robbers?

Am I encouraging all and sundry to start chasing murderers?

No - that's definitely not what I am advocating in my tale.

The story is included merely to demonstrate once again, how incredibly lucky we were.

I was lucky when the thief lost faith in his own abilities and no longer believed he was capable of outrunning a pensioner.

I was lucky when I saw the tip of his foot underneath the car.

I was lucky when the locket was found.

I was lucky when My Saviour and Mrs Christmas arrived on the scene because I couldn't have held the thief much longer.

I was lucky the police believed my story rather than the thief's, although as I pointed out at the time, I would have to be incredibly stupid to attack a nineteen year old who was bigger and stronger than me.

And as I have thought many times since the incident, I was incredibly lucky that the thief didn't have a knife.

Yet I also learned one other extremely valuable lesson that day.

I learned that the human body is a wonderful thing and it doesn't always matter how old it is, as I proved during the first hundred yards of the chase – Ok I was running on adrenalin but it was my own adrenalin.

So even if you are in the autumn of your years; don't give up, go and enjoy yourself and if you are like me – a pensioner – well all that means is that you have more time to indulge in all the things you wanted to do whilst you were working.

So disregard work, it's finished, put all that behind and immerse yourself with what you really want to do and always remember: -

"It's never too late to see,

What you might have seen,

And it's never too late to be,

What you might have been,

And it's never too late to do,

What you might have done,

And it's never too late to win,

What you might have won."

Of all sad words of tongue or pen, the saddest are these, 'It might have been." *– John Greenleaf Wittier.*

"And you might get lucky now and then – you win some." *- Mark Knopfler*

"What time did the Mole Catcher say he was coming for another attempt at removing our Mole, Mrs P?"

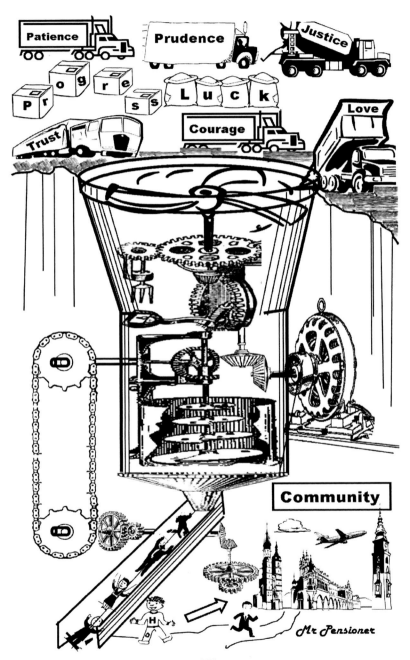

Thank You.

Thank You for the time you took,

In reading my little book,

It wasn't done for the money,

But to try and make life funny,

It was written at my leisure,

To provide a little pleasure,

But if you like what I've penned,

Inform a friend, so they can spend,

And hopefully - you'll start a trend.

There is a delightfully varied cast of secondary characters....and all, even the "baddies" are portrayed with empathy — reader report - Welsh Books Council.

Hektor

Anka

Kyba & Jay

My Saviour

Mrs Cross

George

Justin

Mobile Man

Mrs Xmas

Mr & Mrs Reggie

Mr Cross

Gunman

Stout Lady

Mole Catcher

Thief

Joe down at the club

167

For the "Tentative Buyer"

or

The person who's, "Just Looking".

This chronicle is ironical and sometimes even comical,

Each page tells of a stage, we plan for in old age,

It muses and amuses, so don't make your excuses

Just choose it, peruse it and hopefully enthuse it.